Alex Andronov is a writer who lives in the UK. He is currently working on 7 novels, 5 film scripts, 2 plays, 2 TV series, 1 history of the United States, 1 travelogue and trying to find some focus.

www.gamboling.co.uk

THE BOOK
WITH THE MISSING FIRST PAGE

and other stories

© Alex Andronov 2007

Printed and bound by lulu.com
Designed and typeset by Katherine Hall

ISBN 978-1-84799-121-8

INTRODUCTION

I've often wondered why I write. I know I can't help but do it, but I'm still not sure about why. I wish I could say that I do it for you, dear reader, but primarily I do it for me.

Every day I wake up with a new idea, at least one new thought for a story, and if I don't write it down then it plagues me all day. Mostly I simply jot down the bare bones, but at least once a week for about the last three years I've turned one of them into a story. These stories have been published on Mondays and Fridays on my blog gamboling.co.uk over that period. Not all of them have been good, but some of them have sustained me over the years.

On the one hand I don't mind if nobody ever reads my words. I write because I have to. But I also want to create the best story for anyone who happens across it. For Socrates, the unexamined life was not worth living. For me unread fiction isn't fiction.

I couldn't have made this book without two of my dearest friends. If you don't like soppy bits then skip down to the last paragraph of this introduction.

Katherine Hall is the love of my life. She helps me achieve everything that I do. And this book is a testament to her more than anything else. She wants me to be happy, and I want her to be the same. Together we are able to encourage each other in our pursuits. In this particular project Katherine also was chief proof-reader and type-setter and she also helped with the selection.

Nick Ollivère's writing has been a constant source of encouragement over the last fifteen years, every time he gets better I am determined to try and keep up. If Nick didn't write I probably would have lost confidence years ago. Nick helped with the selection and proof-reading of this book.

I would never have made it this far without my brother Pete who always said "tell me another one", my mother who always told me how proud she was, and my father who wanted to be sure the story was actually good before committing to it. If I hadn't been taught from an early age that the story had to actually be interesting then I don't think you'd have this collection in front of you. Ellen and John are my greatest fans, and I thank you for making my parents happy.

Finally thanks to Adrian Lightly, Dei Treanor, Kris Stewart and Joe Brett who have all been good enough to put up with my testing stories on them for so many years. And especially Kris and Adrian who very kindly helped with the final proof of this book.

This bit is important. If you like this book then I am shamelessly asking you to help me, I want you to go online, to lulu.com and buy a copy as a gift. If you don't like this book, just take a second to think about somebody who might. If the answer isn't "no-one" then please pass it on to them. I know this is a bit gratuitous, but this book is supposed to work on word-of-mouth publicity, so don't keep it to yourself.

Thanks for reading,

Alex Andronov
25 October 2007

CONTENTS

The book with the missing first page	11
Party	13
Cross words to say	15
A game of cat and mouse	27
Left out in the cold	29
The exam	33
Expedition to the centre of the brain	35
Dining al fresco	42
It's late	44
Oswald	46
Shrugger	48
Rooting around	49
"Why do you look so lonely?"	57
Deckchair of death?	60
Scorching	62
Voices	68
A star	70
Love	72

Grass	74
Pirates!	75
Poisoned	87
Soup	88
Are we going out?	89
Moon miners	91
Jenna was not happy	97
It's the night before the night before her wedding	100
Does the name Pavlov ring a bell?	102
You know the feeling	103
A meeting in the park	104
The influenza adventure - a Citron investigation	106
Cat's eyes	114
Trapped	115
"I think that's probably it for me"	116
In my kitchen	119
Sarah	121
Important at the time	130
Jake Turnweed	131

THE BOOK WITH THE MISSING FIRST PAGE

A tear leaked out of his eye, rolled off his nose and hit the title page of the book. That just made things worse so he placed the book back on the side table and looked forward and blinked a lot.

He took a sip of the wine and realised that it tasted salty. He wondered why, but then he felt another tear hit his top lip and he knew. He never usually cried, in fact he hadn't for years. He knew the exact date, or rather the last time he had cried. He started thinking about it, and then he stopped. He consciously thought, loud enough in his head as though he'd said it, "no point raking over old coals." He tried to think about other things. Like how lovely his setting was. He'd arranged it all so that he could be found properly. So somebody would walk in from the hallway and see this kindly old gentleman (which is how he viewed himself and was actually accurate) reclined in an armchair by the fireplace, with a glass of wine, a bottle and fresh glasses within reach. But they never did come in, they hung around in the hallway and in the kitchen and in the dining room. Blast them, blast them and their continuous music and standing up.

And anyway, he thought, who would talk to him now he'd been blubbing? He probably looked really drunk. And anyway he had this theory that young people thought he was dead most of the time. Why did he have to go and find that book? Out of all of the ones on the shelves. There were so many to choose from, but it was his memory. It was starting to confuse things. Why hadn't he realised it was that book? The book with the missing first page?

Alex Andronov

Even now he hated that boy. It was a blank page of a book. Why should it have mattered so much? But it did. Now every time he reached for his wine glass he saw it again.

He contrived a move of his body in the chair that would absolutely ensure the book fell on the floor. And it did. But it fell open right in front of him, displaying its wound. Celebrating it almost.

It had been almost seventy years since it had been ripped out. But the scar was just as severe today as it had ever been. That boy had forced him to give up everything. His tuck, his magazines, a slingshot and a Dan Dare badge. It seemed like nothing now, but then those were all the things that were his, and he took them all. The boy had taken everything that defined him. And all he had saved was the rest of this book. It was the only thing the boy had allowed him to keep, and he hadn't dared show it to anybody. Because the scar revealed far too much of him.

The book with the missing first page

PARTY

His moustache drooped unnecessarily into his champagne. He turned away and once he was sure she was no longer in eyesight he spat the champagne into a flower pot. Sadly his moustache went with it and Michael spent a furtive couple of minutes digging around in the now wet soil, dry the moustache, find the glue in his inside pocket, reattach the moustache to his upper lip and wipe the soil from his lapel with a linen napkin.

Once all of this was over with, Michael decided to mingle. He sidled up to a beautiful woman. On his way he picked up a glass of champagne and a glass of whisky from a passing tray. The woman looked impressed, made eye contact saying, "hello stranger".

"I thought you were supposed to say that to people you knew but haven't seen in a while," Michael said.
"You sure we haven't met?"
"Looking as beautiful as you do, I'm pretty sure that I would have remembered you. Have we met?"
"No I was just fishing, fishing for compliments."
"Really?"
"Works every time"
"Well I feel such a sap now."
"So are you going to give me that champagne or not?"
"Sorry, here you are, but I don't know how you can drink that stuff."
"What champagne?"
"No that stuff specifically. It's fucking awful as far as I can tell."
"I don't mind it. Don't hate me."

Alex Andronov

"I won't hate you simply because you don't share the same taste in champagne as me. What an idea!"
"I just wondered if you were one of those guys… You know those guys who absolutely hold their own views. They believe they are right all of the time and if you don't agree with them you're not just wrong, you're actually stupid."
"Going out with one of those guys?"
"Was just dumped by one actually."

Just then the music at the party changed pace from some kind of schmaltzy waltz to something a bit faster. Michael decided to pick his moment.

"Do you fancy a dance?"
"Why not? I like this song."

She looked at him very closely for a second. And then chose to move in close to him so she was resting her hand lightly on his chest. "Can I ask you to take off your moustache though?"
"How did you know?"
"Well if it wasn't for half the guys in here tonight wearing fake moustaches it would have been pretty hard to guess, except that there's a lot of glue on your face."
"And you still want me to take it off?"
"Yes, please."
"Spoilsport."

The book with the missing first page

CROSS WORDS TO SAY

You may have seen a cakewalk, but have you seen plenty of this? (9)

Jenny was looking out of the window and it was definitely snowing. Jenny had told her mother that the news had said to not make any unnecessary journeys and that it was definitely snowing but Jenny's mum didn't think it was true.

"But that's what they always say when it gets the slightest bit cold. 'Avoid unnecessary journeys' like your life should revolve around something as random as the weather. And anyway," she said clearing things up, "it's not even snowing".

But it definitely was snowing, and Jenny wasn't sure how well her mother would take it. Jenny knew that her mother had to go to work and that they all thought like her that a bit of weather shouldn't stop her from getting in to work. But what about school? Somebody at school had been saying that if it snowed the school would be closed. Jenny thought about this for a while because mentioning it now if the school was open might just make it seem like she wasn't cooperating. She had been the one to bring up the snow in the first place. And it wasn't as if she didn't want to go to school either, she liked school, it just seemed that none of the people at school liked her. She was just worried about what her mother would say after they'd driven there in the snow and found it closed. Especially if she somehow found out that she'd known all along that it was a possibility.

Alex Andronov

But before she could think about this anymore, Jenny heard the light scrape of keys against the post at the bottom of the stairs that meant that her mum was leaving. Jenny hopped off her seat, picked up her satchel and headed for the door. She knew better than to dawdle, the alarm would be on within seconds, it was definitely time to go.

They got in the car and drove. Jenny wanted to listen to a special CD that she'd selected. Her mum wanted to listen to the news. They sat like normal, not talking. Jenny liked it when there was music on because you were kind of allowed to talk. But if there were people talking on the news then you weren't really allowed to talk.

As they drove, the snow was falling thicker and was settling more thickly. And they were driving more and more slowly until finally they simply stopped. It was not for want of trying but something had happened in the engine and it wasn't going to go anymore.

"What are we going to do? Nobody ever drives along here." Jenny's mum said rather presumptuously. Jenny wanted to say that it couldn't possibly be that they kept the whole road open only for them, but she had to admit that she had never seen any other car drive down this road.

They sat for a while until the battery stopped working and the radio died. It was suddenly colder the moment the fans stopped blowing hot air in their faces. Jenny already had her coat on which was lucky because when she wasn't wearing it, it lived in the boot. And she would have been very cold if she'd had to go out to get it. Her mother calmly picked up her coat from the back seat. And then rather uncalmly tried to put it on without standing up. But when her mother had picked up her coat something had caught Jenny's eye. Underneath it was nestling today's paper.

"Maybe we could do today's crossword".
"I've done it already".
"Oh," Jenny was disappointed, she always liked doing the crossword with her mum.
"Well there's one clue that I haven't got."

The book with the missing first page

"Oh," Jenny suddenly perked up, "what is it?"
"It's, 'You may have seen a cakewalk, but have you seen plenty of this?', it's nine letters."
"Hmm," I don't know.
"Mmmm," me either.

Jenny and her mother waited for an hour, and nobody came. After a while Jenny started shivering. And a little bit later her mother started doing the same.

"What will we do if nobody comes?"
"Somebody will come."
"But…"

Suddenly a light reflected on the front window from behind. Another car was arriving. It slowed and a guy jumped out.

"Are you okay?"
"Yeah, just, our battery's out."
"Okay I'll give you a jump."

The man walked round to the front of the car, and opened the bonnet. But before he'd looked for too long he came walking back to the window.

"I don't think it can be your battery. What happened?"
"We were driving and the car suddenly slowed, and stopped. Then after a while later the fan stopped running."
"Well that makes sense. You've got a hole in your radiator. The battery must have run down trying to keep the two of you warm."
"So will we be able to get it going again."
"Not without a tow-truck. I'm sorry. Can I take you somewhere where we can call someone?"
"That would be great. Actually the only reason I'm here is that I'm trying to take Jenny to school."
"Actually me too, my son's in the back in there," he pointed to his car, "Tom keeps telling me that school is cancelled for today. But I'm not

sure exactly how that helps me. If he can't go to school then I can't go to work."
"Tell me about it."
"Look, should we try and drop them both off and then see if we can call somebody from there?"

Jenny and her mother abandoned the car and got into the jeep that belonged to their knight in metallic silver. As she got in the back Jenny was sitting next to a boy that she didn't know. The boy spoke.

"Are you Jenny?" he said.
"Yeah, how did you know my name?"
"You're in the year below me."
"Oh I…"
"You're new, aren't you?"
"That's right, but I…"
"People have been talking about you." He clearly realised that it sounded bad, so he said, "nothing bad, they're just interested because you're new."
"Do you do crosswords?"
"Um. Sort of. My dad taught me I think," said Tom.
"Yeah, my mum taught me."
"Why are you asking?"
"My mum has a clue that we can't work out in today's crossword. You haven't done one already today, have you?"
"No."
"Not at all?"
"No, we usually do the Saturday one."
"Oh. Well the clue, this one we can't get is 'You may have seen a cakewalk, but have you seen plenty of this'. It's nine letters." Jenny realised right after she'd said it that she'd almost been doing an impression of her mother when she was saying the clue.
"I think I know the answer."
"What is it?"
"Well, I think it must be 'Abundance'. Yes that must be it."
And somehow, with the half-smile of the realisation of the joke in the

answer, accompanied with the steely determination of his jaw that he would in the end be right about what he had just said, even though he was overly polite about it in the way that he described it, Jenny loved Tom in that moment. Even though she had no real idea of what love really meant or if this, as such, was it. She knew that this was something, and only years later would she realise and tell people that she'd fallen in love with Tom from this moment.

Love Handle (3, 4)

In all towns there is one bar which is the coolest bar to hang out in. This is true everywhere, even in the big cities. Especially in the big cities. You might think there are several or that it all depends on your individual taste, but in that case you've sadly, tragically almost, missed the point. Cool isn't about what you think it's about, it's about what other people are doing all the time when you're having a rest. But in a small town it's easy. It's clear. And in a small university town it's so easy that even deeply uncool people can figure out where it is. And this was what Tom was thinking as he watched Jenny walk into the bar.

Jenny was wearing thick-rimmed glasses and had her jet black hair tied back in such a way that Tom was sure that later in her particular story she would take off her glasses, and let her hair fall to her shoulders in a moment designed to make the viewer say, "oh she's actually beautiful". But Tom could see perfectly well that she was beautiful now. He could also see, as she dropped a small bag of tangerines on the table and they all started rolling off in different directions, that she was quite clumsy.

The two of them had been kind of avoiding each other since the beginning of the year. They had ended up at the same Uni by accident. And really the only tension between the two of them was that they had once, when too young to know what it really meant, said that they would get married. They had just come off stage from being Mary and Joseph in the school nativity and they had been asked one of those fake adult questions that no child has ever really thought about. The adult asked if they had ever thought they could be married and that is when it happened.

Alex Andronov

They had said that they would definitely get married and that they would be best friends forever. And that had been all that it took. The adult mentioned how cute this news was to all of the other adults and from then on they could never really escape from this statement that they didn't ever understand.

Jenny, who had thought about this a lot, had decided that this was the reason they hadn't been able to stay friends when they hit puberty. This was not something that would have happened if they had simply been friends. In that case it would have been easier. But being betrothed to somebody who is changing that fast is tricky. Especially when you're changing just as much. Tom just thought they'd drifted apart.

They'd been going to the same university for a year and a half now and still they hadn't really acknowledged each other's existence beyond more than a quick nod or hurried "Hi". And Tom had noticed and logged in the back of his mind with a sense of embarrassment that he had had a different girl with him every time they met. And Jenny had logged in the back of her mind that she had been alone every time that they met. She was alone again now.

Tom wasn't, however, with a girl but neither was he alone. He was with some guys. They had just come from a lecture and had folders, books, scarves and beer bottles littered around them. He looked over to Jenny who had everything neatly packed away. On the table in front of her was a glass of white wine, a coaster, a pen and a newspaper.

Tom got up and walked towards her. As he made his way over he realised that she was deep in thought and probably wouldn't notice his arrival. She was looking down at the paper and a lock of her hair fell off of her forehead and down in front of her eyes. She pushed it back up, ran her fingers along to the ends and tucked it behind her ear.

Tom arrived at the table and pulled out the seat opposite her. She suddenly looked up with panic in her eyes and almost started to say something before she realised who it was and simply said, "Tom".

The book with the missing first page

"Hi Jenny," he responded, "how are you?"
"I'm okay. You?"
"Yeah I'm fine."
"What made you come over?"
"Well I just saw you there and I thought I'd say Hi."
"Bullshit!"
"What makes you say that?"
"Well we've seen each other a million times and you've never come over before."
"You weren't alone before."
"I was." This was the moment that Jenny softened to him because although she'd been obsessing about this information clearly it hadn't been important to him. But then she also thought badly of him again because he hadn't been properly paying attention to her.
"Oh," he said, "well I wasn't alone probably. And so… Yeah…"

He took this moment to actually sit down on the chair he'd been gripping since he wondered over.

"Okay," he said, "it was the newspaper. That's what made me come over."
"Oh charming!"
"No! No. I meant something better than that. I meant… It reminded me of when we first met. And I suddenly thought that it would be so much better if we could just first meet again. And pretend that there wasn't any of that history there. That I could just kind of come over and as friends we could work on the crossword together."
"I see."
"Yeah, that's all I was thinking. I mean it's not as if we ever did the crossword together again after that very first day, so it wouldn't be something from the past or anything. So what do you think Jenny? Couldn't it work?"
"Well I've actually only got one clue left. But maybe. Maybe that could work. But…"
"What?"
"You can't call me Jenny anymore because that's from the past too. Everyone calls me Jen now."

"But… Couldn't I just have that as my pet name for you?"
"Well maybe… Oh damn you!"
"What?"
"That's it! You just got it. The clue was Love Handle (3, 4) and it's Pet Name!"
"Well in that case you'll have to let me call you it!"
"We shall see."

And at that moment, as a waitress walked past and Tom ordered a bottle of whichever white Jenny had been drinking, she felt that feeling again. And it was delicious.

Break one's word (9)

Tom was eating his cereal while Jenny dithered in the kitchen. It was Christmas Eve and the goose was… Well it wasn't getting fat, Jenny thought, because by now it would probably be dead. And anyway they were having turkey again this year. This had caused a bit of an argument in the flat over the last few days. Jenny had wanted to try goose for a change but Tom had put his foot down. He didn't usually mind about things like this so she knew it was important to him. But she also knew that she'd pushed him to defend himself. It was probably destructive to play the bad guy just to see that reaction. But she wasn't able to help herself.

She hadn't been able to help herself at the work Christmas party last night. She had known it was wrong but she had done it anyway. It was a moment of weakness and she was already trying to tell herself that it didn't mean anything. She had slept with a guy. It had never happened before. And she knew it would never happen again. But while she would easily be able to get away with what she'd done she also knew that she didn't want to. It wasn't that she wanted to go out with this guy. It wasn't that she didn't want to go out with Tom anymore… No actually that was it, exactly it. She didn't want to go out with Tom anymore.

She looked back at him sitting at the table. He was just pushing his cereal

The book with the missing first page

bowl away from him, and pulling the paper closer to him.

And then he said quite quietly to Jenny, "here's the one I can't do, 'Break one's word, nine letters'".

Point of resolution (5)

Jenny was sitting in her kitchen and it was snowing again. It didn't seem to snow that often anymore at Christmas. Not actually on the day anyway. But there was still a week to go. It was getting dark out there. She had a box on the table which had contained her outgoing Christmas cards. "Ho Ho", she thought to herself, "they probably are more outgoing than me". She looked at the box and it still had one more card in it. Of course it did. It was a card she'd bought twelve years ago, two years after she'd left Tom, and had always meant to send to him. It had a picture of Father Christmas doing a crossword on the front. But she never had sent it because… It never seemed enough. And because she had left him at Christmas it had always seemed likely that he wouldn't really want to hear from her. And then after a while sending it had seemed much less important.

But she had seen something in town which had made her change her mind. She'd put it off for about a week but now, this evening, with the snow starting she'd decided that she would send the card after all. And there was still time.

She picked up the card and inside wrote:

> Tom,
> Your Answer: Hyphenate
> My Question: Amundsen's forwarding address (4)
> Meet me there, 7pm, Tuesday if you're interested in catching up.
> Merry Christmas even if you're not.
> Jenny x

She sealed it, addressed it and walked out of the house. She didn't even wear her coat as the post box wasn't far. She walked, hearing the slow crunch of the pebbles beneath her feet. The crunch was slightly faster on the way back as she realised just how cold it actually was. She got back inside and tried to shake some of the snowflakes out of her hair. But they were already melting.

On Tuesday she got ready early, and then sat around waiting. When she got there early she realised that it was probably a mistake. She hadn't even bothered to look at what the place was like inside when she had seen it from the street. She had just picked it because the name was the answer to one of her favourite crossword clues. Or in fact because it's name had reminded her of the clue, and in turn it had reminded her of Tom.

The bar was okay, she supposed, but it was clearly designed for the younger clientele. They only had two kinds of wine: white and red. But actually when she started to drink the glass of white it wasn't as bad as she had expected.

At five minutes past seven he arrived. And a flood of relief flowed through her. She had been sitting there for the last five minutes imagining him looking at the card and laughing at the thought of her sitting in the bar alone.

He walked up to her, and looked at her glass. It was empty and she knew immediately she'd given away the fact that she'd been early. She looked up at him and he said, "red or white - that's all they have".
"White please".
"I'll be right back".

As she sat there waiting for him, she wondered what they would actually end up talking about after such a long time. She'd got as far as planning on them meeting, and worrying about if it would work, but had stopped short of working out what it would be that they would discuss once they got there.

He ambled back to the table.

The book with the missing first page

"So you figured it out did you," she said.
"Yeah, we'll it's 'mush' isn't it. Although the fact that I've made it here lets you know that, I suppose." He grinned. And then he looked a bit more serious before going on, "I can't believe it's been so many years and we're still setting each other clues like this."
"Yeah, it's weird isn't it?"
"Here's one, 'Overloaded Postman'".
"Oooh, um how many letters.?."
"Loads."

They both laughed at the silly joke and it lightened the atmosphere a little further.

"So," Jenny said getting down to it, "are you doing anything for Christmas"?
"No. Not really."
"What does that mean?"
"Well it means that I haven't really planned anything. I've got some food sorted out - sort of."
"Ah," she said.
"What about you?" he looked up and made eye contact for the first time in a few moments.
"Well I've got all the food sorted out but I haven't got anyone to share it with."
"You know you really hurt me before."
"I know."
"And I've not really dealt with that."
"Okay. If you don't want to come that's fine."
"No," he said, "I'd love to come but…"
"What is it?"
"Well, if I come you have to promise me that you don't ever do that again. It's now or never for committing to me."
"I can do that, I've always loved you since the moment we first met. I was just confused I think. I won't hurt you again."
"Okay."
Tom sat there thinking for a moment and then finally said, "Pixel".

25

Alex Andronov

"What's that?", Jenny asked.
"That's what this is as a clue. A 'Point of resolution (5)'."
"It is, but Tom."
"What?"
"No more games now. This has got to be real this time."

The book with the missing first page

A GAME OF CAT AND MOUSE

Harry is sitting next to his mother in the shoe section of a giant department store. It's the first time he's been allowed to sit down all day, spending most of it being dragged round the different departments. It was all so very boring. Except the hat section, that had been fun. His mum had told him off a lot but nothing serious. Now that he had sat down for the first time he started feeling a little sleepy. But even been tired couldn't explain what he saw next. A large mouse and a small cat were fighting over a piece of cheese. The thing that struck Harry immediately as odd was that they were fighting with swords.

Harry quickly hopped off his seat and ran over to the skirting board. He knelt down beside them and simply said, "Wow!"

But soon his "Wow" turned into "Ow" as the cat accidentally cut him on the knuckles.

"Keep back," the mouse shouted out, "I'll defend you".
"You can talk!" cried Harry.
"You can see us!" cried the cat.
"And, just think," said the mouse, "if you could stab him like that then he could stab you back".

This was clearly such an unsettling thought that the two of them stopped fighting and looked up at him.

"What are you doing here," asked the mouse?

Alex Andronov

"I'm shopping," said Harry.

"But this is a department store," said the cat, "boys don't shop in department stores."

"No, my mother's shopping, I'm just with her".

"But," said the cat, "that happens all of the time. And the shop never lets kids see us."

"He's bought something, must have", said the mouse, "that's the rule. Kids can't see us because they don't buy anything, parents can't see us because they are never concentrating."

"But I haven't bought anything."

"But you've definitely done something different," said the cat.

"I did try on a hat," admitted Harry sheepishly.

"Aha!" said the mouse. "That must be it."

"Incredible," said the cat, "to think that this hasn't happened before."

"Indeed," said the mouse, "Well I'm afraid I'm going to have to complain to management. What kind of system is it where we can be discovered so simply? Eh?"

"I know, I just can't believe it. I'll come with you - I have got to see the look on his face when you tell Cuthbert what's happened."

"So, about this cheese," the mouse said as they started to turn away from Harry and towards a hole in the skirting board.

"Shall we split it?" said the cat?

And with that the cat cut the cheese in half with his sword and gave one half to the mouse, and popped the other half in his mouth. After chewing for a second or two he said, "One half in my mouth, the other half in my mouse" and the mouse and cat started laughing. In fact they didn't stop laughing until they were well out of sight.

Harry stood up, turned around and walked back to the stool next to his mother. He would say something to her - but he was sure she wouldn't believe him.

LEFT OUT IN THE COLD

The boys were out again, Edward could feel it. Perhaps it was because it was just a little bit too quiet. Or maybe it was the way the boys indoors were looking at him - as though they all had a guilty secret they couldn't talk about, but that they desperately wanted him to discover. Whatever it was, the boys were outside again.

Edward understood the attraction of it, the attraction of being out of bounds. When he had been a boy it had been smoking they had all wanted to do. And in those wonderful summer days hiding in bushes, running through meadows and accidentally setting fire to Colin (an eminently combustible child) the teachers were always after them.

But now it was different. The world was cold. Everyone knew that. The ground had been frozen solid ever since scientists had tried to reverse global warning in the early twenties. Well they had succeeded in their own way but only by creating global freezing. And now it was minus seventy in the summer. And nobody even went outside anymore. Nobody who valued their extremities anyway.

So why were these boys doing it? Why were they going out? Edward knew there was only one solution. He'd have to follow them outside.

***

Despite all of the protection, the cold crept quickly around his skin. The hairs all over his body stood to attention faster than a lieutenant who has dropped his rifle in front of his drill sergeant. Ah, what a simply sublime simile, he thought to himself as the cold air cupped his balls and forced him into action.

He stepped forward and heard nothing, his ear defenders stopped any noise. He would have crunched through the snow, but instead he merely walked.

He looked down at the snow for clues. He had hoped to follow the footprints but it was snowing now and it was so bad he couldn't even see his own feet.

What was he doing out here? He could die. If he couldn't see his feet then he might not even be able to get back into…

He turned around and all he could see was the door he had just come out of, it was ajar. He hadn't left it open. He was sure he'd closed it. Just then the door closed from the inside. He ran towards it. But he knew. He knew even though he hadn't heard it. He knew it would be locked.

He walked towards the door. He had to check. It could have just blown shut, he thought. He walked forwards and pulled the door. He thought he felt it move for just a second but then nothing. It was secured.

He turned away and looked across what he remembered had once been a rose garden but now was just a completely plain white vista that stretched on as far as he could see.

He knew exactly where he was and yet he was lost. He wanted to shed a tear but he knew it would instantly freeze and would cause him more trouble than it solved. Instead he gulped down on the air, and regretted it instantly as the freezing vapour entered deep within his lungs.

He looked longingly towards the old school. It looked abandoned rather than thriving with all of the windows boarded up like that. If only there was a way for them to see him, he thought.

And then it hit him. In the dining hall there was a giant glass window that was left. Years ago they had seen wildlife despite the snow. Polar bears and rabbits and so on but now even they had migrated further south, the temperatures being too cold even for them. Right now he couldn't help wondering, why hadn't he?

A stupid thought though. It was still too cold for him to survive down there. It just would have taken longer to die. He had to concentrate. No time for stupid thoughts like that. If he could get to that window he could survive.

He stumbled forward. He hadn't quite realised how far away the dining hall was from the door but he supposed it was all a question of diameter versus circumference. It was very different to be walking inside a shape than all the way around it. He kept his mind active by trying to do the relevant maths in his head.

After twenty minutes he was cold and tired and not nearly far enough around. He was finding it more and more difficult to put one foot in front of the other. Soon enough he stopped. And after a second he fell to the floor.

As he lay there he remembered a common room meeting twenty years ago. There was a big debate and then it was decided that the lock should be removed from the door. There was no point because there were no burglars. But they had worried that somebody might accidentally get locked out. In fact he had recently thought about adding a lock to stop the students from getting out but hadn't for just this very reason. Such a fool! Why hadn't he remembered this before? His left cheek was starting to get wet from the snow he was lying on. So why couldn't he open the door? They must have been on the other side holding it closed.

What was it? Righteous indignation? Or having been a teacher this long? Whatever it was the rage that bubbled up inside him, and more than that the desire to tell the students off awoke in him, an energy he didn't know he had.

Alex Andronov

He leapt up, dusted himself off and started almost running towards what he now knew was an unlocked door.

The book with the missing first page

THE EXAM

She walks into the room, in a bit of a rush like everybody else, but also trying to feign some kind of laid back appearance. She absentmindedly rubs her left palm against the side of her other hand. An ink stain from last minute revision has left its mark. She's not even consciously aware that she's embarrassed in case anyone realises that she has actually done some preparation. She finds a desk three-quarters of the way down the hall, on the opposite side to the door.

Two pens, a pencil, a protractor (for some reason still in her bag from the maths exam), an eraser (she didn't like to call it a rubber because it reminded her of an embarrassing joke somebody had made about something she'd said back in middle school), some tissues and a sweater, which she hung over the climbing bars that were next to her desk.

The girl in front of her had three teddy bears and a troll. For a fraction of a second she wished she had something to personalise her desk with. And then she remembered what she thought of people who did that.

She sat for a moment trying to decide if she was nervous. The boy next to her was opening his mouth wide enough until it clicked over and over again. He looked bored. Was he faking it?

The back of her neck prickled. The noise of slowly moving footsteps was coming towards her. A flop of paper landing on each desk. Face down it would be. Sitting there on the desk. Face down. The footsteps are at the desk behind her now. The kid behind is looking at her rather than his

33

paper or the invigilator. She can feel the look, it's making her face hot. Her face feels suddenly very warm, like she's being suntanned from the inside. It's that damned kid looking at her. She'd be okay as long as he stopped. The footsteps arrive. So does the paper. Flop. All she can see are the words "This page has been intentionally left blank." Her face goes cold and the top of her head feels like it is mid-way through a massage. Which rather than being relaxing is merely unsettling.

It had taken the invigilators ages to get to her table. She still has time. She looks up at the front of the gym. They've finished laying out all the papers already! Somebody is writing out the start and end times. There are forty seconds to go. 39. 38. 37. 36. 35. She tries desperately to remember her candidate number. 31. 30. 29. 28. 27. If that boy clicks his jaw one more time she'll kill him. 20. 19. 18. 17. 16. 15. 14. 13. She adjusts the jumper on the bars. 7. 6. 5. 4. Oh God. "You may now turn over your papers".

EXPEDITION TO THE CENTRE OF THE BRAIN

Day 1

We managed to convince the subject to lie down so that we could enter his ear. He protested at first but we explained that the additional altitude required for even a seated entry would mean so much additional danger money that his medical insurance wouldn't cover it. He lay down and didn't even complain too much when it took Wally three attempts to get the grappling hook into his ear lobe.

We started our ascent. I always tried to go first in these situations because it's the most dangerous time and I like to think it inspires confidence in my group. I got to the top and set up the safety system for the rest of them.

The rest of the group made it up with little incident. I've been looking down at them the whole time. The last one up is the only girl of the group a cute little minx called Julie. I want her desperately but I'm trying to conceal this desire with every fibre of my being. I want to maintain some level of professionalism.

When she proffered her hand as she reached the cusp I helped her and tried not to obviously look straight down her shirt. I swear she wasn't wearing a bra. As she arrived on a sure footing I turned around and saw what they'd all been staring at. The inner ear stretched out before us – giant, dark, terrifying and quite full of wax.

Alex Andronov

Each one of us knew we were about to advance. And we automatically reached out with a torch in our right hand and an ear-bud in our left. Every one of us except Leftie who rather ironically, even though I shouldn't say so myself because I came up with it, is the only one of us who is right-handed.

We started off. It was hard work but we had known it would be. And we were all looking forward to the tympanic membrane. The most comfortable place to sleep in the body bar none. I know you'll get some who say it's the soft tissue but that's not for me. Wally, he's the most technology savvy of the group, he's got an artificial membrane at home. He swears by it. And one time although he lives quite a long way from me I went down to visit him. I said I was doing some shopping locally but he knew I'd come to try out the membrane. It was nice. I mean it was good even. But it wasn't quite the same. All the time I was lying there it kept making me think of the real thing and how this wasn't as good. And while in my mind I was thinking about how many more jobs I could pick up to get me back to where I was heading right now, Wally was explaining just how difficult it was to look after.

We slipped as quietly as we could into the tympanic area. Once there we could talk again. Just not by the cavity. It won't damage anything, and I know some do but I think it's unprofessional. Quite often we're going into the brain to deal with a mental problem anyway. Giving them voices in their head doesn't seem like the greatest of ideas.

So we've arrived - base camp for day one. We're all tired and I'm just writing my journal as I see one by one each lamp go off. I'm sure Julie looks over at me for a moment before she turns her lamp off. I wonder if I'll dream about her. Right that's it for me. Just a quick oatcake to help me sleep. And then bed.

The book with the missing first page

Day 2

I was the first one up this morning. I feel fabulous. That great feeling of having really earned your good night's sleep. I worked hard and slept well. I only had pause for a moment when I realised I couldn't remember if I'd had any dreams. Nothing came to mind, just a general elated feeling. No specifics but I was feeling… I was sure it was a good dream. I wondered vaguely if it was about Julie.

Once everyone was up and had eaten breakfast we started on the main work of the day. We would need to head to the brain as soon as we could. We started off. The aim was to get the information and hopefully back to the ear again tonight. Sometimes it takes longer at the brainface than that and then you have only an hour or two back at the membrane before leaving. But missions were never longer than three days since the Spiegelman incident. Now these things were so routine that nothing like that could ever happen.

It took us most of the morning to reach the brainface. At this point we usually liked to split up into pairs as it speeds things up. As chance would have it Wally and Leftie decided to go off together leaving me and Julie as a team.

The thing with this job is that really only one of you can work at a time in a region. Julie wanted to go first. She was still new to the game and got a kick from experiencing all of the subject's emotions. I mean I'm not saying that it doesn't affect me, of course it does, you wouldn't be a nanobot if it didn't. But over time you do get more used to it. Anyway I was quite happy to lie there on a soft mound watching Julie probing away. She was chatting away about all the stuff she was experiencing, the sound of her voice was just tinkling away. It was, I don't mind telling you the happiest moment of my life up to that point. But what happened next now holds that honour.

Suddenly Julie stopped talking and started giggling. She was laughing and smiling. And as I looked up all over her face was a look of unbelievable joy. I knew exactly what had happened but I could scarcely believe it. It was so rare. She had hit an endorphin stream. She was completely off her head on happiness!

She stepped towards me, rather wobbly at first. But soon she was walking right over to where I was half lying, half sitting in stunned statuesque silence.

"I know something about you," she said. Her eyes glittered like they were finishing her sentence in semaphore.
"Oh, do you?"
"Yes. You don't think I know but I do."
"Oh, what's that?" This part wasn't the happiest bit of my life. In truth I was quite nervous at this point.
"I know you've, how should I say, taken a shine to me."
"Ah… I can explain…"
"You don't have to explain. I reciprocate. I fancy the pants off of you."

This bit was the happiest bit. I was quite pleased with myself. Now for this next part I must draw a delicate metaphor over the events. Suffice to say that we knew each other.

Much later the voices of Wally and Leftie came to our attention. We dressed hurriedly. And I don't think they were aware of what had happened. Then with a mounting sense of dread they reminded me of the time. It was so late. There was no time to get back to the ear tonight. It was already one in the morning. We would have to camp by the brain.

We were in trouble and I knew it. I felt very guilty but I also felt like it was worth it for what had gone on that afternoon. In fact I felt guilty for that thought too.

I'll need my oatcake to sleep tonight. I am so uncomfortable internally and externally it's impossible to imagine that I'll sleep at all tonight.

The book with the missing first page

Day 3

I woke suddenly and desperately thrashed out in the darkness. There was, of course, nothing out there. It was the end of my dream letting itself out into my awake self.

We had to start moving immediately if we were going to make it out. Even now it will be a miracle if we get out. The food supply was dangerously low.

We started moving. After a few hours we were at the membrane, tired, hungry and very dispirited. Once we got to the ear the few spirits that remained deserted us. The subject is sick. He's blocked up. His ear is completely filled with wax. Normally this would delay us. But normally we would be facing this almost half a day earlier. And not while tired and hungry.

But we cracked on. We had to. What other option did we have?

It was hard, demoralising work. Each break we took I sat a bit further from the group. They know I'm to blame. Well Wally and Leftie just suspect. Julie knows. She was off her head. I shouldn't have taken advantage of the situation.

I'm writing this on what I know is my final break. In the next few minutes we'll be through to the connection to the nostril. I know what I have to do. I have to take the plunge. I'll pretend to fall down the Eustachian tube. I know I won't survive. But I know the extra supplies will help my group. So I must do this. Eventually my body will work its way through our subject's system. But I will be quite dead. It may be some time.

Alex Andronov

Day 4

I can't believe it was an accident. And I don't really know why I'm writing in a dead man's diary.

I can't believe I just admitted he was dead. I wasn't sure I believed the others until I just wrote that. Now I know that I know he's dead.

So what was I writing? Oh I was saying I didn't know why I was writing in here, except, I suppose I do. I was going to write that I thought it wasn't an accident. But now I know it wasn't. He knew he was going to fall down the Eustachian tube. He was trying to save us. And it might have worked.

We are making good progress. It's easier on the bigger rations but it's harder without him.

We used to call him Captain Oates after all those oatcakes he used to eat each night. Now it doesn't seem like the best way to refer to him. His real name was Lawrence. Although I never heard anyone use it. He told me what it was last night. After the first time we had - what was his phrase - known each other.

I'm not sure if I should write this part. This next bit. Because, well, it doesn't make me look very good in the company's eyes. Or anyone's. I'm scared to write it but I have to.

I faked it, I faked the endorphin rush.

I just wanted an excuse to break the ice. And it seemed the best way to do it. I never meant for anyone to be hurt. I promise I never meant for any of this to happen. And now I'm as scared of getting out and facing up to what's happened as I am scared of being stuck in here forever.

The book with the missing first page

Epilogue

Four nanobots went in and, yesterday, three days later, three emerged, tired and hungry with many stories to tell.

Today, while having my breakfast, Captain Lawrence Oates fell out of my nose and into my cereal.

This journal is dedicated to Lawrence, the bravest nicest nanobot I ever had the pleasure to meet. I hope he's gone to the great tympanic membrane in the sky.

Alex Andronov

DINING AL FRESCO

Uncle Jack went toddling off towards the bar for a quick schooner and the rest of us visibly exhaled.

It had been, what had become, an exhausting afternoon. First Walter had arrived complaining that he was absolutely appalled that we were proposing to dine al-fresco. He predicted precipitous precipitation. But his god-awful lamentations had been nothing in comparison to Uncle Jack.

He had arrived half-cut and had proceeded to apply the metaphorical scissors to himself.

After pinching almost every girl's bottom (an event which was made all the more embarrassing by his refusal, point blank, to pinch Gertrude. Despite her placing her, not inconsequential, posterior within inches of his hand and bellowing "pinch it or I'll tell Monty". Monty, whoever he was, must have been dead - or worse deaf and married to old Gertie - because he didn't respond despite a call put out for him that some said could be heard over three counties. I've heard many things said about Gertie, and I've said a few of them myself, but I won't hear a word against her lungs. And you wouldn't hear a word if you were against them either.), Uncle Jack had set his attention towards the bar, and now as he returned an incredible thing happened.

Walter, he of the doom-laden phraseology, was proven correct as it started spluttering down. Walt, it must be said, looked rather chipper for a man who had just been given the beginning of a light soaking.

The book with the missing first page

"I told you all," he cried, "didn't I? I did, I think you'll find, tell you all."

Just as Walter was regaling us with stories of barometers he had encountered, and apparently simple tests you can perform on common seaweed, I noticed, out of the corner of my aspect, old Jack bumbling with his bumbershoot. Just as he found the automatic opening button, the magnitude of his problems became apparent. He pressed it and the device damn near exploded. Metal and plastic flying this way and that. And Jack standing there cursing to the heavens shouting, "I ordered this as a whisky not a whisky and water."

Jack was a man who feared dilution, and that is how I remember him best; standing, screaming at the sky for want of something, anything, to cover his drink.

Alex Andronov

IT'S LATE

It's late, or at least it's late for you. It's past your bedtime. The room seems more alive in the dark than in the light. You get up, turn the light on, and then get back into bed and look around. That's the curtains that are swaying, that's the door to your wardrobe that's casting a shadow over your bed from the light above the door. You try and remember it so that when you turn the light off it will all seem normal. You get back up and turn the light off. You jump back to your bed just in case there is something hiding underneath there. It's okay when you get off quickly because then whatever it is, is as surprised as you are and the light's on. But when you're making your way back the thing will know you need to get back into bed. You jump back in and look around. It's okay now. You can make out what is the curtain, you can make out what is the wardrobe door. It's all okay.

But jumping back onto the bed has had repercussions. They've heard you downstairs. One of them comes up to check on you. You can hear the steps approaching. You close your eyes tight, pull the covers up and try hard to lie really still. One of them - it sounds like dad from the footsteps - comes in. He notices the window is open and goes over and closes it and re-arranges the curtains. He walks over to the wardrobe and closes the door. He murmurs "Goodnight" under his breath, and then walks out of the room.

You sit bolt upright, look around the room, and again everything seems to be moving towards you. It all seems a lot closer than it would in the light. If the window is closed, surely the curtains wouldn't be moving.

The book with the missing first page

So what is that coming towards you? Something shimmering and hissing coming towards you like a sheet. If the window is closed it can't be the curtains! What is it? You leap out of bed and run towards the light switch hitting it just in time to see... Nothing... There was nothing there. The window just wasn't closed properly, it was just the curtain. You can hear your mother calling up from downstairs. Urging you to go back to bed. But will you turn off the light? You know you're just being silly. But... But... But... You can't help it, tears leak down your face and run salty into your open mouth that's already whimpering and the heat of your cheeks heats your tears and makes your skin tighten. A lump in your throat rises, you know it shouldn't you're big and grown up, but it comes and once it reaches your mouth, you're bawling and all you want is your mother to come and rescue you. From what? From what doesn't matter, you just want to be reassured, you just want a night light in your room.

Alex Andronov

OSWALD

Oswald didn't like it when people noticed he was different. This was a shame for Oswald because it happened all of the time. Oswald only had one eye and it was smack in the middle of his face. His eye was just above his nose. And people couldn't help but stare whenever they saw him.

He had tried to make friends but even the loser kids all shunned him. He had tried to get good at sports so the other kids would like him and pick him for their teams. But it was hard to practice for team games by yourself and Oswald's depth perception had never been that good.

If he ever tried to be smart in class the other kids just hated him more. There didn't seem to be anything poor Oswald could do.

Then one day Oswald was sitting in his English class. English was his favourite class. In fact English was everyone's favourite class at his school because the English teacher was Miss Greg. Miss Greg was a very very attractive young women. At Oswald's all-boys school you just had to be female and have a pulse (pulse optional) to attract attention and yet Miss Greg was genuinely foxy. She was a tall, blonde, willowy and she had a slight eastern European accent that Oswald had never been able to place.

So it was English with Miss Greg. They were all paying minute attention to everything she was doing and saying. But despite paying that much attention they could hardly have noticed the draw string of Miss Greg's dress getting inside the book she was reading to them. And that when

The book with the missing first page

she closed the book the string was inside the book. And that when she picked up the book the string was still inside the book. And that when she lifted the book above her head to make a point about something her dress became undone. Suddenly the boys could see everything. Miss Greg realised immediately what had happened, but was so surprised that she didn't immediately cover herself. She just stood there - stunned.

Everyone was silent. Nobody was saying anything. And then Oswald said, "That's a sight for sore eye". And everyone laughed. Even Miss Greg (and then she quickly covered herself).

Alex Andronov

SHRUGGER

A man is standing on a platform eating a croissant and drinking a bottle of Coke. He looks bored and he doesn't seem to notice that the flakes of the croissant are falling down his jacket.

A woman walks up to him and asks him if this is the right platform for somewhere. He doesn't even listen to the end of the sentence and when she finishes speaking he doesn't even react. She starts getting louder as though speaking louder will get him to understand. In the end the man just shrugs his shoulders and the woman walks off not knowing if he didn't understand the question, if he didn't know the answer or if he just didn't care. That's the problem with shrugs, they can haunt you for the rest of your life.

The book with the missing first page

ROOTING AROUND

It had been a month, and Sean knew it was time to go up into the attic. He had been avoiding it since he moved in. It was a complete mess up there. Why hadn't he paid more attention to that estate agent's check list? The old man hadn't been required to clear it, and now it was all just up there, sitting there. Somebody else's stuff that just hadn't been wanted any more. He had tried to motivate himself by watching "Cash in the Attic" and "Antiques Roadshow", but Sean just wasn't that lucky. He knew it would just be useless junk. He wasn't even interested in it.

He went to the fridge and took out another beer, returned to the couch and sat there trying to decide why he was so unlucky. He knew the answer, it was all her fault. It was easier just to blanket blame her for everything. It was her fault that he was here in this house that he didn't really like. It was her fault that he was sitting on the couch drinking beer at 11 in the morning, and that he had time to watch daytime television like "Cash in the Attic".

But he had been trying hard, really hard, not to think about her. And he had started to wonder, just recently, if perhaps this effort was part of the problem. Perhaps if he stopped and actually thought about her, if he thought through why it had happened then he might not have to think about her anymore. Whereas up until now, every time she surfaced in his mind he would bat the memory away. It seemed to be every few seconds she would occur to him.

He would look at the way the cutlery was arranged in the drawer and know that Jennifer wouldn't have arranged it that way. He would look at the way his living room looked like a dentist's waiting room and know that Jennifer would never have laid it out that way. He would look into the fridge and know with a vague nagging sense that raw meat and cooked were supposed to be on separate shelves, and one was supposed to be above the other, and know that he'd been told a thousand times but had never bothered to really remember. And he knew he was certainly doing the washing up wrong, but couldn't remember why.

All he knew, all too well, was why he was in this state. Sean had introduced Jennifer to his boss, and that was it, she had left Sean for his boss. This was the short truth of the situation. That was all of it in a nicely packaged single sentence. A single thought. If only he had never introduced them! Then none of this would have ever happened. They had been happy before that. Well sort of. But if they'd never gone to that stupid office party then none of this would have happened.

Could he have done more to stop it? Could he have tried to win her back? Maybe he could but he didn't realise that she was going until it was all far too late. She had already fallen in love with his boss long before Sean had ever realised that she had had fallen out of love with him. And what wasn't to love about him? Tony was a sort of perfect man, he had money, a great car, knew the good places to go to dinner, was cultured and knew about the theatre and stuff. And he was sporty. He didn't know as much about movies as Sean, but then that might have been something that Jennifer appreciated about him.

She was always asking him to stop analysing movies in the car on the way home. It wasn't fair, they had used to love talking about movies when they first started going out and now what, she wanted him to change that as well? He'd changed too much for her already. He'd started putting the toilet seat down, he had worn shirts with collars, he'd done the washing up without being asked, he'd even not sworn when her parents were round for dinner. What more did she want? She wanted him to take down some of his movie posters and stop talking about movies as much? He could understand the other stuff, he knew he had just been getting away

The book with the missing first page

with stuff before, stuff that he shouldn't have been doing anyway. And actually, once he tried it, even he could admit that he looked better in a shirt with a collar. But this stuff was different. This was changing something about him. But that's where it had started to go wrong. He should have resisted, but he couldn't.

He had decided to surprise her, to do something different. So on one movie night he started getting ready like usual, but when Jen had come in to ask him what they were going to see he presented her with the invitation he'd been given at work. It was an invitation to a swanky party. He got them all the time, not that he told Jen, but he never went. They were a perk of his job, he just didn't like them.

He told himself that he didn't like all of the smoke and noise. But that wasn't true, he loved all of that, he feared parties because they required him to make small talk, to make polite conversation with people who never had anything interesting to say, to listen to them babbling on about how they got there, what the traffic was like, how well they are doing in their boring, pointless jobs. And then to hear himself doing the same back to them. He hated all of it, he was afraid of it. He saw it like some kind of gladiatorial challenge, the challenge being could he think of something to say in time for when the other person stopped talking. Every time there was a pause in the conversation, his heart would start pounding, as though it was keeping count of how many seconds had been silent. Fearing the shame, fearing the silence and especially fearing the inevitable moment where the person would say something like, "right well I'm going to mingle, I'll catch you later" and then wander off.

He feared them also because of the attractive women who would be flirting just feet away, not necessarily with him, but close enough. They made him sweat and he was sure they could smell it. And now it was worse because when he was with Jen, he felt that he shouldn't look, and that she would see him looking or even just think he was looking. So now he just kept flitting between men, staring at one of them, and then violently snapping his head to the next guy trying to avoid even resting his eyes for a second on any of the women, even though he wanted to. Then he'd start worrying that Jen would think he was a gay and he'd start sweating again. So, taking Jennifer to a party instead of a movie was a big move for Sean.

And that's where it all went wrong, thought Sean. He finished his beer and put it in the recycling box. Some things, he thought, had stuck. He liked the recycling box because it was like the beer walls that he used to construct as a student showing off how much beer they had managed to consume in a weekend. The box showed how much beer he'd drunk in a fortnight. Same idea.

Something about the word boxes triggered a memory in Sean's mind. He remembered all too suddenly that he was supposed to be clearing the loft. Okay, he thought, I can do this. He went upstairs, opened the hatch, lowered the ladder and went in to the loft.

Sean dragged himself up through the hatch and into the attic. He stood up and found the light switch. He'd only been up here once before, but he'd already worked out that it was a really stupid idea of whoever it was to put the light switch up so high that you couldn't reach it from the ladder. It was bad enough coming up the ladder, but going back down in the dark was particularly hair-raising.

What this room needed was a particularly good clean. That's what Sean would have done if he was keeping any of this stuff, but this stuff was all going to be loaded into the back of Sean's car and taken to the dump. He'd get all of the stuff out and then he could work out how to clean this space. He turned around slowly trying to take in the sheer amount of stuff that was here. How many trips to the dump would it take? Ten? Twenty? Far too many.

He looked at the floor and realised that it was completely covered in dust and grime. He shifted a pile of boxes to one of the clear spaces and saw, as he had hoped, that the floor under the boxes was relatively clean. He climbed over some of the boxes and sat in the clean space he had made. It was like he was in the kind of fort that he built as a child. It felt relatively safe and reassuring. Since he'd moved into the house he'd never really seemed to be able to fill it enough. He'd always thought that this sensation wasn't to do with the amount of stuff that had turned out to be Jen's - he hadn't been able to take with any of that with him. It was more about there not being another person. The silence of somewhere empty is deafening. It's partly the way that no-one else is speaking but it's mainly the way that every time you return home everything is in exactly the same place that you left it. When he was living with Jen he had resented the fact that she kept moving everything; now he knew he missed that.

But maybe there was more to the amount of stuff side of things. There were, after all, some rather strange spots in some of the rooms downstairs. There was an empty room that really looked like there should be a dining table in it. And in the living room the fact that there was only a tv and a single-seater arm chair certainly hinted at being alone. But for the first time, Sean thought as he settled in between the boxes, he felt safe.

The fluorescent bulb was creating a shaft of light that fell just a few feet in front of Sean, and as he looked through it he could see all of the dust particles dancing. He watched them fly in every direction and it was very peaceful. It was truly distracting. He let out a giant sigh as he slightly decompressed, letting go of a very small part of the stress that he'd been carrying in between his shoulder blades for the past few months. As he exhaled, all of the particles of dust sped up, and moved in different directions. And he watched as they slowly came back to their normal non-interrupted pattern and fell again as they had before he had disturbed them. He was very tired, he hadn't been sleeping well at all, and now as he looked at all of this around him he started to feel very sleepy. His eyes slightly lost their focus, but then something attracted his attention, and he was wide awake.

Just beyond the shaft of light, there was a box which had some writing on the side of it. The writing was in professionally printed lettering, it said, "Time Machine".

Sean was fully awake now, looking at this box. Could it actually be true?

Alex Andronov

A time machine? It seemed so far fetched. He suddenly realised he'd just been sitting there staring at it. He tore his gaze away from the box for a second. He tried to digest what it could really be, or even if it was real. He looked back, it was still there. He was so unsure of what it could be that he wasn't even sure that it would still be there when he looked back. But it was. The box was still there tempting him. Still there reaching out towards him. Calling him to use it. But should he?

When would he go back to? That question almost seemed impossible to consider. It almost wasn't worth a question, the answer was so obvious. He would have to go back to that night - the night that he took Jen to the party. Could he just stop her from meeting his boss? He'd surely be able to convince himself to not go. He could remember how nervous he'd been to go to the party in the first place, so surely it would be easy to convince his old self that his worry was founded.

But what would happen if he didn't take Jen to the party? Sean suddenly realised that the only reason he'd decided to go to the party in the first place was as a last ditch attempt to keep Jen. So maybe it wouldn't save them. Or at least he'd have to come up with something else really brilliant. But what could he do? Anything he thought of instantly gave Jen the chance to hook up with somebody else. Maybe the problem had come earlier in the relationship?

Perhaps he should go back earlier and convince himself to be more considerate. Maybe if he went back to the very beginning then he could make things better. Make things right for Jen from the very start.

So it was decided. He would go back, maybe an hour before he met Jen, and tell himself what he needed to do differently. And with that decided, he got up onto his knees, shuffled forwards and touched the box.

Somehow Sean had expected something to happen from just touching the box. Like it would innately be able to read his desire and take him where he wanted to go. But nothing had happened when he touched the corner of the box, other than the realisation that the box was made of cardboard

The book with the missing first page

rather than wood as it had seemed in the half light of the attic.

He saw that some tape was holding down the flaps on the top of the box, and he started to pull it back towards him. His knees felt very uncomfortable in this position so he sat back down, but kept very slowly pulling the tape towards him. Sitting back down made some of the blood rush back to his head. With this he realised that he was actually quite drunk. Was he ready to meet his previous self and explain to him how he should change his life?

And maybe it wasn't such a good idea anyway. Suddenly Sean wasn't so sure he wanted to go through with it. He would have to stop being himself to win Jen, and he wasn't sure that he was totally ready to do that. Sean quite liked being Sean, and at this point he wasn't sure he didn't like being Sean more than he liked Jen.

And anyway, surely he didn't have to travel through time immediately? That's one of the beauties of time travel, you've always got a chance to do it again if it didn't work out the first time. Maybe he'd have a coffee first and sober up? And maybe a shower wouldn't be the worst of ideas.

The only downside to this plan was getting out of the attic, as the light switch was not within reach of the ladder. But, he thought, he'd be back up here in a little bit, maybe he'd just leave the light on when he went down this time.

As he stepped down the ladder the full force of daylight re-entered his eyes. And he found himself blinking more than normally. Everything looked so normal. Up there everything had seemed so surreal. It was like coming out of a cinema after seeing a film during the day.

He walked downstairs and into the kitchen. Oddly he couldn't find any coffee in the cupboard, actually there wasn't anything in the cupboard which he was sure wasn't right. He walked into the living room, and realised that there was completely different furniture in there.

Alex Andronov

"Hello," said a voice from an armchair that Sean didn't own. It was the old man Sean had bought the house from.

"Having fun travelling through time?"

The book with the missing first page

"WHY DO YOU LOOK SO LONELY?"

"Why do you look so lonely?"

"I don't know, maybe because I am lonely", the lonely-looking guy said, looking up from his beer. He slightly chuckled to himself in a way that sounded like it meant the subject was being closed.

Helen continued to stare at him as he looked back down at the bubbles forming on the top of his beer. The brim of his hat touched the rim of the bottle. She made a decision.

"What's your name?"

He started to answer, he opened his mouth to do it. But before he could say anything he was seized by a smile. A grin really, and she knew from that grin that he was a good guy.

"Bill. Bill," he paused to chuckle again, a slight half chuckle which told Helen that, if she could have seen his eyes, they must have sparkled at exactly that moment, "my name's Bill. What's yours?"

Bill looked up and turned. He still didn't look quite at her. But he certainly was paying more attention to her than his beer. As if to redress the issue he lifted up his beer bottle and buried its neck somewhere under his moustache.

"I'm Helen." She thought for a second. And then another. She knew through both of these seconds that it would be possible to go with this man. This man that she found attractive, this man that she could love. But for every second that she remained thinking about it she knew that it couldn't happen. Consider, she considered, the practicalities of the situation.

Could she really go out with a guy now? Especially a guy that she'd just met. She knew that the longer she thought about it, the less likely she was to do it. And she knew that she'd keep thinking about it until it was no longer a possibility. She was her own worst enemy, and she hated that. But at the same time she knew it was her best defence. If she could just keep herself thinking then she didn't have to commit.

Why was she so bothered? She'd not gone out with people so many times before. And she didn't even like men with moustaches. The only thing that bothered her was the realisation that not going out with people was easier in the short term but that easier in the short term almost certainly didn't mean happiness in the long term.

It was something that Helen had been thinking about more and more recently. That the things that gave her the most happiness in the short term - drink, drugs, sex - were very rarely related to long-term happiness. In fact every single thing that was an easy way to be happy today was an easy way to be miserable tomorrow. And the opposite was true too, the things she was most proud of in her life had been really hard. They really took an effort, but she had never looked back on an effort and thought that she had wasted her time.

"I sound like a PBS special".
"What?" Bill looked confused, and suddenly he looked directly at Helen. "What did you say?"
"I said, I sound like a PBS special. I had had this whole conversation in my own head. Like it could have been in somebody else's head I guess, but there it was in my own head, and then at the end the next thing I needed to say to myself was to tell myself that I was sounding like a PBS special, but unfortunately I thought that thought too loudly and ended up saying

The book with the missing first page

it out... well to you."
"I like PBS, and I like you."
"Okay, well I like you too, so what are we going to do about it?"
"Well I'm going to buy another beer right now. Just one more but I'm going to do it. And I'd like to buy you a beer too. Or whatever it is that you'd like to drink..."
"Beer's fine."
"Right, well I'm going to buy both of us a beer, and then we'll just see how that goes. But there's one condition".
"What's that?"

"I want you to talk about who you are. Because I'm interested in who you are. But I need to know from you before I buy you this drink, that when you talk about you, you won't sub-vocalise anything. You'll just tell me exactly what you're thinking. Because while you might think that what you're thinking is the most embarrassing thing in the world, to me it's the most interesting thing you can say."

Alex Andronov

DECKCHAIR OF DEATH?

We wheeled round the corner and then came to a sudden stop. There was a man, a young man, sitting in a deck chair by the side of the house. The most important thing we had to do was discover if he was a stranger. That was paramount. Because if he was a stranger then we would have to cycle away as fast as we could.

There was a slight bias in our questions to each other. If there was even the slightest hint that this young man wasn't a stranger then we would be free to investigate.

"Have you ever seen this man before?" I decided to cut right to the core of the situation.
"Define 'seen'."
"Well, the Oxford English dictionary defines 'seen' as…"
"No, no, not all that again. I mean…"
"What can you mean? Either you've seen him or you haven't. Simple logic there, no grey areas, nice and clear."
"No, it isn't, that's the point. That's why I started all of this."
"So what pray is the point then"? I tended to get more fruity in my language when my dander was up.
"I haven't seen him per-se but I have heard talk of him from my Aunt. She was talking about a man very much matching his particulars just yesterday and I would say that she must have been talking about him".
"How sure are you that this is the same man?" My interest was piqued, we might have a chance.
"She was talking in shock about his shoes, and telling my cousin (your

The book with the missing first page

sister) in no uncertain terms not to trust him because of them".
"Why shouldn't you trust these shoes"? I asked, they seemed to me to be perfectly ordinary shoes.
"Well," my cousin said, "just you look at the lining of the shoes, it's purple. That, your mother said, was a sign of an insatiable appetite".
"But he's not a fat man, he's pretty slim".
"That's just what your sister said, but apparently, your mother said it wasn't that kind of appetite."
"Well I'm sure I don't know what she's talking about".
"Neither did I, but your sister and your mother started giggling when they said it. I felt it best to clear out".
"Good move".

We both just stood there looking at this insatiable thin man sitting possibly dead in the deckchair, wondering at things that had been said that we couldn't understand. And knowing that there were so many unknown unknowns out there that we knew we'd never know. And while we were standing there looking at him, a fly flew down onto his top lip and wandered along and walked right up his filtrum and into one nostril. A second later the chap sneezed and the fly flew out again.

But the sneeze had proved one thing at least this chap was still alive. And so, just in case his mysterious appetite involved eating small boys, we were off, cycling away into the sunset.

Alex Andronov

SCORCHING

Steven lay on a slab of boiling hot concrete. He was wearing only his shorts and a damp towel on his forehead. He had never thought that he would have picked the concrete to lay on but the deck chair was made of plastic and it had started to feel like it was melting. He didn't mind sunburn but he didn't want plastic burn.

He moved his hand to the side and found his beer without looking. It was floating in a bucket of ice. He pulled the stopper out and then took a pull of the beer. It felt cold along the length of his body for a few glorious seconds. And then he put the stopper back and gently dropped the bottle back into the bucket.

They'd all taken the piss out of him when he'd first suggested the stopper. But now they were all doing it. It was the only way to keep the beer afloat in the bucket of ice. They'd all been coming here for years. In fact they'd never even been able to use a bucket of ice because the bottles would so easily turn over once open. But Steven had changed all of that.

Life had changed for them all since Steven had blown in. For Steven it was a change from life back in dreary old England. For everyone else it was a reminder that they had all come out to Spain to finally enjoy their lives and not just to die. Steven drank more than everyone else, had more sex than everyone else and caught more sun than everyone else. But more than anything else he used his brain more than anyone else. It was this that had made him a sudden celebrity, and had got him the sex.

The book with the missing first page

But despite outward appearances to the contrary, Steven was not satisfied. Steven was hungry for more. Steven had a single secret in his life. A secret that he never told anyone. Steven had never, in his whole life, ever been satisfied. And that was the thing that made him want more than everyone else. And when he saw something, like he had seen that woman across the bar yesterday, nothing would stand in his way. Nothing.

He would have to have her.

***

Steven blinked his eyes open and closed, and open and then closed again. He couldn't tell the difference. It was really dark. Dark and quiet. It was so quiet that Steven could hear his eyelids opening and closing. Forget pins dropping it had to be really quiet before you could hear stuff like that.

Steven had been lying on his left arm for quite a while. First it had fallen asleep, then it had done that gentle tickleish pins and needles thing. About half an hour ago there had been massive amounts of shooting pain up and down it. And eventually that had stopped too. Now it just felt dead.

But through all of that time he hadn't dared move. Steven was not alone in the room. Steven had been lying under the bed in which the woman he desired and the guy who currently seemed to be ringing her bell had been hard at it. He'd felt safe to move while they had been distracted but he had been right in the middle of rearranging himself when they had finished. After that they had just lain there cuddling quietly. But eventually they had got up and gone. Or rather that was the thing. Steven could have sworn that only she had left but he couldn't hear any breathing but his own. He decided to risk it. He moved his arm. Or rather he tried to but it wouldn't move. Steven rolled over, which isn't easy under a bed and then used his other arm to shake the dead one. Warm blood rushed back into his arm and the pain returned. It felt like there were little pieces of glass in his veins. As the pain rushed through him he asked himself the fundamental question, "was she worth it"? To which the answer was still yes. In fact she was more intriguing now than before.

From the moment that he'd woken that morning he had known today was the day. He'd risen, dressed and walked straight over to her villa. He'd knocked on the door and they'd started talking. She seemed interesting and interested. And so Steven had invited her out for breakfast. But she had given the perfect response. She'd invited him in for breakfast.

It was while they were toasting the bagels that this other guy had arrived. She had told him to hide which seemed promising to Steven. As he was legging it up the stairs he decided that she was only getting him to hide because she wanted to have sex with him.

So Steven had gone and hidden under the bed of what had seemed like the spare room. But of course that was the room they had decided to use.

His arm felt just about useable. He listened again. Still silence. He decided to risk it. He slid himself out from under the bed and stood up. He had a quick glance back at the bed just to be sure. And that's when he realised that there had been something else dead in the room other than his arm. It was the man in the bed.

***

Steven didn't know what to do. He turned around a few times hoping that by the time he turned back the guy would suddenly be alive. He decided to stop being silly and besides he was getting dizzy. He stopped and looked properly. There didn't seem to be anything obviously wrong with him other than the obviously uncomfortable angle in which he was lying and the fact that his eyes had rolled back in his head. It looked to Steven's untrained eye like he'd had a heart attack. Well the sex had sounded pretty amazing. Just as he was trying to decide if that would be the way that he wanted to go he heard a noise on the stairs.

"Gloria, don't come in here a second."

The book with the missing first page

The steps stopped coming for a second and then they started again.

"Steven?"

She walked round the corner, saw what had happened and then fell on the floor. She looked back up at Steven from all fours. Steven suddenly realised she'd gone into a kind of attack style crouch.

"What," she snarled, "did you do to him"?
"Nothing. I was going to ask you the same question. He must have died just after you left the room."
"Oh," she said looking instantly more relaxed, "really"?
"Of course. Why would I want to kill him anyway? I don't even know who he is."
"Yes but maybe you thought you would have to kill him to sleep with me?"
"I don't think so. I'm sorry, you're lovely and everything but to kill for? Well possibly, but I'm not sure this guy was ever going to find out about us. That certainly wasn't my plan."
"What shall we do? Hide the body?"
"Why? We didn't do anything. We should just phone the police, explain what happened and everything will be fine. I promise."
"No we can't phone the police. We can't."
"But," said Steven, "if we just tell them the truth then nothing will go wrong, nobody did anything."
"No," she said, "I think I might have killed him."
"You can't have."
"No, I think I did."
"But you'll go to prison."
"I can't I can't."
"But I can't lie to the police."
"You have to, you must. I… I… I'll sleep with you if you will."

That was Steven's dilemma. He knew that she was the woman, out of all of the women that he'd ever met in his life that he most wanted to sleep with. She was the one. She was so beautiful. So young, fresh and pure - or at least she seemed that way. He thought to himself, I don't care if she thinks she's killed somebody. "Why should I care?" he thought. And then he thought about himself, thought about himself and decided that this was certainly a risky situation.

***

Steven put down his beer and turned himself over onto his back. He knew that he was supposed to towel off the sweat when he turned over. But he couldn't be bothered today. Apparently it meant you got an uneven tan. But he couldn't be bothered today. Today he didn't have time for it, he was playing catch-up.

He'd had to spend all morning with the police telling them what had happened. He'd told them the truth. All of the truth. And they'd believed him. They had even understood why he hadn't come straight to them. They too were men. They too had often thought, when they saw Gloria that they would do anything to know her. He had had to spend the day, and the night with her. He made promise after promise to her while they ate, drank and made love. And yet there was no way he was not going to tell the police about the dead body in the master bedroom.

Steven turned slightly onto his side so that he could drink some more of his beer. The slightest breeze caught his chest and made a shiver run down his back. He was transported in his mind back to England. Cold rainy England. He didn't want to go back there.

He wasn't sure what to tell people. The real reason sounded like a laddish lie and so he thought about telling people that the reason he turned Gloria in was because he feared having to go back to England. That he feared being deported.

He thought it sounded better than the truth. That it sounded more reasonable than the reality. The real reason he had turned her in is that despite many attempts to improve things, Gloria was singularly crap in bed. Steven lay back down on the sun lounger and used the chair in exactly the

The book with the missing first page

way that the name suggested, he lounged in the sun.

He couldn't shake one thought from his mind, "and people thought I was going to grow up".

Alex Andronov

VOICES

He sits on a train. He has slightly spikey gelled hair but when he leans forward to read his book you can see he's beginning to thin on top. He's reading to distract himself not just from all the people listening to music and jabbering away, he is reading to distract himself from his own head - from his own voice.

The train goes round a corner and squeaks in a rather alarming way. He looks up distracted for a second and even in that moment he hears his head say, "you're worthless". He puts his head back down and tries to focus on his book. But he's lost his place and his eyes are wandering all over the page. The voice is getting louder and more cross while this is happening. It is simply, for once, just repeating the same phrase again and again. Once it used a word he didn't even know, which made him feel really bad. He'd always wondered afterwards how that could be possible. But he still hadn't quite brought himself to look it up, it might be too depressing.

Suddenly there was a hand on his knee, a woman's hand. He followed the arm up and saw a beautiful face looking at him - really examining him. She looked into his eyes and he blinked.

"Sorry," he said, "was I in the way?"
"You," she paused and looked excited, "fascinate me"
"Me?" he resisted the urge to look over his shoulder.
"Yes you. Every day I see you and you never seem to see me. Every day you're reading and when the train squeaks you look up, and then

you always look so worried. I've started worrying about why you're so worried."

"I…" the words wouldn't come, the voice started swearing at him in his head, but he ignored it and looked at her. He'd never really seen anyone as beautiful as her before in his life. Maybe in a magazine or a movie but she didn't look fake, she was breathing, he could see that. She kept his gaze the whole time.

"You can tell me, I promise, and you don't even know me yet"

It was the word "yet" that convinced him.

"I hear voices," he said, "telling me that I'm useless. Telling me that I can't do anything."
"Well you can't be useless. I think you're brilliant."

What had changed? Something. Something had changed. The voice had stopped. Was it because he'd admitted it or was it because of what she'd said?

"It's stopped," he said.
"Right then, now we can be friends."

Alex Andronov

A STAR

"There it is again."
"What? What am I looking for?"

Melchior was upset, he had just been having a particularly nice dream about a hand-maiden that he had in his employ when Steve had woken him.

He spoke again, putting an upset tone into his voice, "What, am, I, looking, for?"
"A star," said Steve. That was it for Melchior.
"I know it's a star you blithering idiot! If you wake me up in the middle of the night, thrust a telescope in my hand and tell me to look at the sky, I'm not going to think it's a mongoose, am I?"
"Well…"
"Am I?"
"It could have been a comet."

These words had not come from the cowering Steve but had come in fact from behind Melchior completely. It was Balthasar.

"Stop messing around with that poor boy and concentrate on the matter at hand."

Balthasar swooped into the tower. Steve thanked his lucky stars and then stopped when he realised how much trouble that pun would get him in from Melchior.

The book with the missing first page

By this point Balthasar had glided his way across the room to the observation point. With a swift flick of the wrist, his telescopic telescope extended to its full length.

He looked through it and announced "Steve is right. A star is born. We shall follow it. It is moving to its appointed place. When it reaches there, a child will be born. That child will be the king of kings."

Melchior drew himself up and said, "this truly is a great day. I am with you Balthasar. We shall go and worship this infant child."

Steve slowly put his hand up. "What is it now?" asked Balthasar.

"Well I've been making some calculations and it turns out that in fact stars are balls of fire that are millions of miles away. Even the closest one takes four years to get its light here. So if we go and anoint some child that's born there when the star gets to its resting point, we'll have the wrong one. We'll have to work out how far away it is and then find who was born there that long ago. And it could be thousands of years ago."

"Shut up Steve," said Melchior.
"Well said Melchior," added Balthasar, "lets go and find Caspar".
"Yes, I always thought he had a better name anyway."

Alex Andronov

LOVE

She had the word "love" written eighteen times on her t-shirt but she didn't know what it meant. She'd had enough of it; she had been trampled on enough, too much. It wasn't fair when Malcolm had done it but she had been too hurt then. She had just rolled over. And now her kids just kicked her every day. They assumed she could drive them home after their parties. They assumed she'd walk their dog. They assumed she would make them their tea. They assumed she had nothing better to do.

The problem wasn't their assumptions, and she knew it, it was that they were right. She hadn't had a man since Malcolm. She hadn't wanted to at first, and then there was Simon which she had known was a mistake before anything happened. She had no regrets about Simon. His hair had smelt of smoke but she'd never seen him smoking. He was obviously a liar so she let him pay for dinner and then never returned his calls.

Then there had been nothing for a while. And that had been fine really. Until Malcolm invited them all to dinner. He had been banging that bitch Brenda for years of course, but he didn't have to parade her. Didn't have to rub her nose in it. The problem wasn't bitch Brenda though. It was her kids. Everyone had someone but her. They all had partners. Except her. The problem was that there was an odd number of people at the dinner table.

That night she'd gone home and made a vow to change a few things. She pulled out all of her old clothes. She had gone up two sizes since then and she wanted them back. The old clothes that flattered her. To be thin again. To be wanted. To feel good enough that you wouldn't just feel contempt for someone who wanted you.

And a month and four days later she had done it. She'd lost the weight and now she was wearing the shirt. As she looked in the mirror she recognised her 22 year old self. She had the word "love" written eighteen times on her t-shirt but she still didn't know what it meant.

Alex Andronov

GRASS

They are lying on the grass. The two of them. Her in a denim skirt, him in tan shorts. They each have a plastic cup, half filled with rapidly-warming beer. The odd combination of deep bass vibrating you but being unable to hear the melody that you only get at a festival is washing over the whole area. But they are kissing and don't notice.

They roll over each other and giggle. Everything seems possible. They are away from their families. Away together for the first time. For the first time, they don't feel different from adults. But the adults around them feel different. The adults are bored and cynical. As bored and cynical as they usually are, but for a second when they first see the two of them carrying on they think about what they've lost by becoming old. And then they snap back and say something like, "get a room".

The two of them don't notice. They feel adult without feeling like adults and for one day in the sunshine it's the greatest feeling in the world.

The book with the missing first page

PIRATES!

William Marshall was leaning against a wood fence. As he leaned forward the vines came close to his nose. He could see the grapes. They were so bright and shiny that he could see the glint in his own eye within them. Monkeys were running up and down the branches having away with the prime fruit. It was their time, the sun was setting and the people weren't ready to face the evening yet. He gave his beard a deep scratch. As he did it the fresh salt from the days sailing cut into his hand. It was a pain that had seemed immense when he first experienced it forty years ago, but now the ritual comforted him. He always knew he'd done an honest days work when he had salt in his beard. Even if... especially if the day hadn't been honest by other men's standards. He knew what hard work was, and he'd never understood why one job was more honest in the eyes of the law than another. As long as you worked hard to get your money, as long as you worked the hardest to get your money then it must be your money.

A beautiful warm breeze fell towards him, the monkeys were chattering in the trees, and there was salt in his beard. This was the life for him. The only thing missing was women and wine. He turned around and walked into the bar.

Although it was quiet compared to his usual kind of establishment, there was murmuring from the tables. He put it down to the playing of cards which seemed quite intense. He approached the bar and sat at one of the stools.

Alex Andronov

The keep came over, and said, "what'll it be?"
"The stakes must be high tonight."
"Always high here."
"Must be good for business."
"We do alright."
"Lucky you."
"The house always wins, that's what they say."
"That's what they say."

The keep looked at Marshall a bit more deeply.
"You don't know where you are, do you?"
"I'm in a bar aren't I?"
"You're in the most prestigious bar in all of the Windies. The most famous gambling den of the whole sub-continent. You're in Tawnies."
"Tawnies, really? Never heard of it."
"Well your loss," says the barkeep.
"Not really my loss if I'm here is it?"
"No I suppose not."
"Now lets get down to business."
"Betting, drinking or pleasure?"
"Thought you'd never ask."
"Thought I'd never have to."
"Drinking first, pleasure later, and you're to stop me betting at all costs. A piece for you if I've not bet by morning."
"You're on. So what'll it be?"
"Bumbo"
"We don't serve Bumbo here."
"Well I'm not drinking grog."

There was talk suddenly from the nearest table. Marshall heard the word Bumbo being repeated several times.

"We," said the bartender, "don't serve pirates here."
"I'm not a pirate," said the pirate.
"How do we know?"
"Serve me some rum, straight then if you must, but I won't drink grog."

The book with the missing first page

"That doesn't tell me you're not a pirate."
"Check my arm."
"That just means you haven't been caught."
"Yes it does. But if you think you're better than the entire Dutch West India Company then you've got another thing coming."

And just as things looked to be getting ugly, a square hat walked in. Rain dripping off his coat. He walked past everyone who had stopped playing cards and were only staring at him. As he walked past the window lightning cracked highlighting what was left of his face. He made it up to the next door stool to Marshall and said, "This pirate causing you trouble? Because if he isn't, then I will."

The Tawnies had a problem. The word had got out. There were two pirates sitting at the bar drinking straight rum. And these pirates had been drinking rum for eight hours straight. The bar had been hoping that eventually they would get drunk enough to go home. But that hadn't happened. Now they seemed like they were moving in.

"Shall we go to the tables?"
"I…"
"Sir," the barkeep was still on duty out of fear rather than anything more noble.
"I… can't."
"No, Sir can't."
"Sir, now are we?"
"I well…"
The barkeep, looked upset, "I was just asked."
"Yes.", Marshall came to the bartender's rescue, "The only bet I'm laying tonight is that I won't bet. If I lose I lose, but if I win then I pay out a piece to this gentleman from keeping me from trouble."
"Marshall!"
"What?"
"You should be beyond such tricks with the staff. You know your destiny is to die at the table. So why do you deny yourself so? You shouldn't deny your destiny."

77

"No. I suppose not Bunby. But on the other hand, if I am to die at the table as has been suggested, I thought it best to avoid as a pastime."
"You can avoid all you like. But you know all that will happen is that you won't have played and enjoyed for years. You'll just have drunk yourself into a self-hating hole, and then while perfectly innocently walking past a bookies one day fall dead over the table. If it is fated it is foolish to avoid it."
"You have a point."
"You're damn right I have a point. Here's two pieces," Bunby threw two pieces at the man behind the bar and took Marshall by the shoulder. "Now we play."

They walked over to the nearest table. The table was full but their presence was enough to suggest to some of the players that it would be safest to cash in their chips and leave. Once they sat down they were dealt in quickly and efficiently but clearly that wasn't enough for Bunby.

"Check or bet?"
Bunby looked at the dealer like he was talking a foreign language. "I can't decide that," he screamed, "what do you expect of me? Barkeep! Barkeep!"

The bartender limped over, looking very worried. He knew he had let Marshall down.

"Barkeep!" shouted Bunby, "I think this guy is trying to gip us. I can't be expected to play straight sober. I think he's trying to dry us out on purpose. You need to keep me and my friend here suitably drunk. Suitably! Do you understand? If we end up sobering our game will be lost. And currently we have no drink. Do you understand? We need to be drunk here otherwise this man will quite naturally cheat us out of all of our hard earned money."

The bartender made to move away.

"Hold up," Marshall said. "There is another thing."

The book with the missing first page

"Another thing." Bunby assured.
"There is another thing?" The bartender seemed less sure.
"It's a private matter," Marshall said.
"It's perfectly valid, and I feel it too." said Bunby. He'd clearly been in the situation before.
"I can only," said Marshall, "bet well if I'm properly stiff. Half mast isn't enough anymore. I simply can't do it. So get me your finest women. Get me them, one for me and one for Bunby here. We can't have relations, we can't Bunby, but we must have them here for the sharpening of the senses they provide. So we will pay them for that not the other."

Drinks arrived seconds later. And after two minutes the finest women of the establishment arrived. They were excited to be there too. To be with a client who would pay to not have sex, this was a big difference. That's why they were the best. One of them had literally unmounted, an d had been swapped out for another girl, because of the unusualness of the situation.

It was that excitement that Marshall thrived on. It was almost like a real date, much more than the sex his wife would give him freely that night.

***

Marshall had never believed in this so-called honour among thieves. What was the point? Thieve or be thieved upon - that was Marshall's whole life.

And he'd been planning to rumble this casino for close to eighteen months. Each time he returned to the island to visit his wife he had walked past the casino and smelt the money. He knew by now how important planning was, but he also knew that he needed to see all of the angles. And so Marshall wanted to see every place for a couple of nights a month for every month for quite a long time before he went in. And at the Tawnies it had seemed perfect. No pirates, not one in all of that time. And yet there was lots of money being traded. Bunby's appearance moments after he had arrived said that there was a reason that pirates didn't come in, and that reason was Bunby.

"Right," Marshall said out-loud and suddenly, "I want a shag. I know what I said, but I'll pay separate for this. And well. I've earned well tonight."

This wasn't strictly true but clearly come seven am some of the girls were ready for a second go. Marshall stood up and three of the girls stood in front of him offering their services.

"It seems churlish to choose. I'll take you all."

***

As Marshall walked back downstairs he found it hard to keep his legs even close together. He'd been given a workout. He was 60 for christsakes, not a good time to discover the wonders of the foursome. He just wished he'd been able to afford the foursome when he was twenty years younger. Although then he hadn't had to pay for exciting sex.

This was the second time he'd though of Margaret tonight. She would understand. She always had. When they made love it was very different than the sex he had had tonight. Making love was a very different thing.

He walked back into the bar, and he turned the stairs. There was nobody behind the bar at this point which was exactly what Marshall had been expecting. He walked back there and poured himself a drink. He left the now open bottle on the counter as an alibi in case he was caught. And then with a simple and practiced motion he opened the till and emptied it into a bag he'd been carrying in his pocket. There was a safe. He knew the combination by now and he opened that as well. Tight little bundles of money lying in the safe, he picked them up and put them inside his coat lining. He now had it all.

He exited the bar, walked round the corner, shouted at Bunby, "How's it going fella?"

The book with the missing first page

The only problem, Marshall realised later, was that he had thought Bunby must be somebody who needed the wool pulling over his eyes. Whereas Bunby had completely separately and independently been thinking of taking Tawnies. So Marshall was surprised when Bunby pulled out his pistol, pointed it at the ceiling and yelled, "I'm going to fuckin' rob you."

There was only one way out. And instead of the quiet exit he had planned it was time to make the situation abundantly clear.

Marshall pulled out a gun of his own and fired it at Bunby, killing him dead. The crowd looked at Marshall as a hero, and he simply walked out of the bar.

He took his winnings back to his wife, and told her that she better take advantage of him as he was putting out to sea in the morning.

***

Marshall gave the order to cast off and they were away. It was an unusual feeling for Marshall to be leaving a port in daylight and one that couldn't happen anywhere else in the world as far as he knew. He had got used to memorizing the port map and not having to rely on visual clues like a normal captain would. But Marshall was no normal captain. He was a pirate captain. And he was very, very good at it. Three, Two, One…

"One and a quarter turns Starboard" he shouted out.

"Aye Cap'n"

Marshall entertained the possibility of scaring a junior rigger by doing the whole thing with his eyes closed. But there was no point. He couldn't convince his old bones to have fun like that. His brain was still alive to the prospect of such fun. But his bones feared his brain.

The bones knew it was best, even in a safe port like Santa Dominique, to keep your eyes peeled.

Alex Andronov

Marshall turned and looked back towards the port. Nothing there. Five, Four, Three… He swivelled back towards the wheel. Two… There had been something… One… Something on the horizon.

"A third turn to Port".

He wasn't even listening for the confirmation. His eyes were searching for that glint out on the horizon. A shape that had made him start. A sail in the wrong place. It was not a normal route into port. It wasn't a tack he'd seen anyone attempt. Or rather anyone else. It was his route into Santa Dominique, his route over the shallow rocks only Marshall had the map for. So either that ship was soon about to go down all hands or something very troubling was going on.

"Wait. Turn back." Marshall shouted.
"Back to port?"
"Back starboard. Belay that last order."
"Yes Sir, Cap'n sir."

Marshall wanted to turn back to face the other ship. They hadn't been plotting that direction. But Marshall was intrigued. He had to see what happened. He wanted it to not be a wreck not simply because it would have been a senseless waste of life, but mainly because he would feel compelled to help. Or at least his crew would. He had control over his crew, but a pirate crew were more apt to mutiny than a regular one. It was something he'd seen, something he'd instigated, too often in a crew. And this was one of those divisive situations. Half the crew would hate him for not helping, half the crew would hate him for helping. Basically the only thing they were united on ended with gold for them. And this had no gold associated. So Marshall hoped it wasn't something like that.

Most other captains would have sailed the other way. He knew that. Certainly all other pirate captains, but he wasn't the rest, he knew a signal when he saw it. Or at least he thought he did. If it wasn't a wreck it was a signal for Marshall. So while he wanted for it not to be a wreck he couldn't see a good way for this thing to finish. Like he would have said

The book with the missing first page

if he could have trusted his crew, he wasn't happy about this, but he had to know, no matter that everyone else would run away.

The ships were sailing dead towards each other now. There was no doubt that he was falling straight into the trap that the other captain was setting. They wanted him, they knew he would sail straight towards them, they knew he would have seen him.

It was that moment that Marshall knew it had to be Coalface Peter.

"Bring me my looking-glass."

Marshall looked and looked hoping for a sign he was wrong. He was a proud man, a man that loved to be proved right. And yet he was also a man who didn't want to fall into a trap. He looked, and everything on the ship looked normal, absolutely normal, a normal that could only mean that it was being orchestrated. What should he do? He wanted to see Pete, he wanted to know that old Coalface was behind it. But he couldn't wait for that. He couldn't. Marshall's men had just been on leave, they had been just sleeping with women, eating and drinking. They would be fat and lazy, ready for nothing, not his usual ready team he could rely on. This was the opportune moment to attack. He should have been thinking of that this morning and yet he hadn't. He never, ever, normally didn't think of the opposition position. And yet... And yet he'd been fucking distracted by fucking a woman. He'd been sleeping with his wife last night for the first time in a year. The first time they'd made bed together. And just as you'd imagine it had been earache from start to finish.

Marshall was still holding the glass to his eye and by the time he saw Coalface Pete disguised as a Merchant Seaman it almost didn't matter. Marshall was already onto something else. Already thinking ahead. Already planning what he could do.

Marshall, quickly went downship, onto the main deck and found his first mate. "Killen, I have a headache," Marshall explained, "you get us back on course".

Alex Andronov

Marshall vaguely heard the, "Aye Captain", behind him as he headed into the Captain's room.

Once there he found the piece of leather he'd been rather unsuccessfully using as a bookmark. He put it between his teeth. Then he unsheathed his sword and stabbed himself in the leg falling back into his bed. The white linen rapidly started soaking up his blood.

Up on deck things seemed to be going even worse. Killen had ordered the ship to turn portwise and the other ship, unseen by Killen, had turned to starboard. Before Killen even knew he was in a battle, cannon were firing upon him. The pirates of the pirates kept turning and turning and firing upon Marshall's ship while Killen was too timid to do anything about it, and through it all Marshall stayed below bleeding.

***

Marshall could hear that the fighting had stopped. He was weak, he was about to lose consciousness. He took his hands down one more time and dipped it into the blood coming out of his leg and poured it back over his face. His entire body was covered with his own blood. And yet nobody had come, perhaps nobody would come and he would die? He knew that he was very close to the line. The most crucial thing now was to tourniquet his leg. He pulled a sheet towards him and tied the leg as tight as he could. He could feel the bleeding stop. Some of the blood kept dripping down his nose and onto his tongue, each drop tasted like a steel blade, metallic and cold.

Footsteps, there were footsteps, he was sure he had passed out. He tried to keep very still but he could feel that he was moving. It wasn't the usual rocking and lolling that came from the ship but instead it was… it was… Marshall dared not open his eyes to identify the feeling, it felt very strange. He heard a grunt from somewhere above his right arm. He was being carried, that's what it was. Suddenly he wasn't being carried anymore, he was airborne. He knew he would have to act very hard to try and stop himself from exhaling air once he landed. He breathed out

The book with the missing first page

before landing so that the air wouldn't be forced out. He felt a rib crack, and then realised that it wasn't his own. His fall had been broken by at least one… no three dead bodies. He was on a pile. He tried to lay still, but he was slipping on his own blood. Then he heard it, Pete's voice…

"These are the dead?"
"Yes sir."
"How many?"
"Ten in total cap'n."
"Right, see to it that…" Pete stopped suddenly mid sentence, he had seen Marshall lying there, "who did this?". Pete pointed directly at Marshall.
"Not I sir."
"I didn't ask whether you did it. I asked who did?"

Pete was stalking back and forth in front of his five lieutenants. Each of them had been in charge of a different part of the attack. They were waiting for him to dispense gold as reward.

"Perhaps I didn't explain to you earlier how important this little conquest was. Perhaps I didn't mention to you how important it was that we kept this man alive. So," he turned to a tall man with a thin moustache, "why did you kill him?"

"I didn't, I swear."
"You were in charge of the fighting men were you not?"
"Yes but look at him. He has blood all over him he must have been killed by a cannon."
"Liar!" Pete shrieked. His sword ran right through the sergeant-at-arms' neck. His thin moustache drooped for the last time and he fell to the ground.
"Although," Pete looked manic now, he could fully appreciate the problem facing him. He was about to be hanged by the Dutch. He knew it. He had promised them Marshall alive not dead, and the fear was great in him.

He continued, "Although, he did have a point. Marshall does have blood all over him." He spun round to face the cannon-master.

At that exact moment, Marshall jumped up from where he was lying and stabbed Pete through the spleen. Blood poured out of the man as he dropped to the floor. Marshall made sure Pete was dead by cutting his throat. He looked up at the men in front of him.

"I am the ghost of Captain Marshall. I am here to avenge my own death. You have nothing to fear if you were not responsible. The only person I needed to kill was Coalface Pete here. At least for the time being." Marshall paused for a second, allowing some blood to drip from his hair onto his face, he knew he must look terrifying. He started again, "I want you to go to the prison and place yourself within, letting the men within out."

The four looked to each other, the cannon-master rubbing his neck as he did. They ran out of the room, fear painted large in each one of their eyes. Marshall wiped the blood around his face in a failed attempt to clean it, he thought of the wonderful waterfall he had found a season ago on one of the southern islands. He put such comforts from his mind, he looked down at the dead. He was looking for someone in particular. Not seeing him there he called out, "Killen! The enemy is defeated, come here!"

The book with the missing first page

POISONED

I can feel it. The poison. It's cold and sharp and I can feel it sluicing around my brain. As the icy liquid curls round the inside of my skull I can feel thoughts being taken away from me. Stolen. Gone. I move my head up and as I do more function escapes. The poison dripping down, edging down to my spine. I open one eye and look at my poisoner. As I look first I see a syringe and a man. But after a second it all becomes shapes. No edges no definition. No memory of what an edge is. No memory at all. For a brief second everything in my head is pure light.

Alex Andronov

SOUP

Arthur's brother Clive didn't eat fruit generally, however I just kindly left melon nearby. Obviously passionate, quintessentially Romanian, somewhat tough, unfortunately verbose, wickedly xenophobic, yet zen, Arthur's brother Clive didn't eat fruit.

The book with the missing first page

ARE WE GOING OUT?

"Tony is sitting there, no... by the bar. He's got that coat on. And he's got two drinks. A pint and a measure of something clear."
"Oh yeah," Stephen says, "I see him."
"Well," says Sarah - regretting the subject ever came up, "we used to go out... I guess."
"You guess?" replies Steve, "what does that mean?"
"Well, we went on a few exploratory dates. I was never sure if we were going out or not."
"You went out. If you go out, then surely, you're going out?"
"No way."
"Well then, explain it to me."
"Well let me ask you this. Are we going out?"
"Hmmm. Well..."
"Exactly."
"But we just met."
"So? By your definition we're out, therefore we're going out."
"But, there should be an amendment."
"Amendment?"
"Yeah. You know. A sub-clause."
"Saying what?"
"That if you're on a first date it shouldn't count."
"Right."
"Right."
"But what about this then?"
"What?"
"Well be quiet for a sec while I explain."

Alex Andronov

Stephen suddenly realised he liked the way that Sarah had said "sec". He was quiet. She went on.

"Well what about if you met for something else? Say like just something, but not a party, and then you decided to just go on to dinner?"
"Hmmm. You met 'out'."
"But then you stay out. You don't ever go out."
"That's a puzzler."
"Yes."
"So is that what happened with you and Tony?"
"Yeah. Sorta."
"So…"
"Okay. We met in the car park picking up our kids and we got chatting. A common friend who hadn't revealed that she knew both of us showed up and started chatting too. We got her to take our kids with her and we went to dinner."
"Oh."

There was suddenly a lot of silence at the table.

"What? What's up."
"Oh. I just didn't realise you had kids."

The book with the missing first page

MOON MINERS

Grandpa Simon was a great big long grey mouse who knew a thing or two. He was old and crotchety and recently he had become quite a bit thinner. He knew he was old, everyone else knew he was old, but did they have to talk about it the whole time?

Simon lifted himself off the straw his nephews' and nieces' descendents had laid out for him and waddled over to the centre of the room. He didn't have to waddle any more, but he knew that those around him would literally think less of him if he didn't. What was he going to do? The moon was dying, the moon hadn't been so green before. It was definitely greener. And the story that Jennifer had redecorated was getting old fast. He needed to get them to do something. But what?

Why didn't they notice that the world around them was crumbling and the only way to fix things was to go back to the old ways? The old ways were hard, the new ways made things easier for everyone. In the old days people would have gone hungry and the moon wouldn't have supported all of these mice. Now mice were freer. The moon was fairer now. And everyone could do what they wanted always knowing that there was a moon shaped safety net underneath them to save them if they never worked again.

It was his fault, Simon had ruined the moon and he knew it. He had been seen as the great saviour. The freer of the masses, but in the end what had he really done? The ruling class had, he had to admit now, known about the problems of balance. They had been eating the moon for years. They had been living off it, enjoying it, but never, ever, revealing its secrets to the masses. But then suddenly one of the masses had got in charge: Simon.

He had been walking alongside a parade, the stink was high at the time, and everything felt like it was leading up to be a great summer when suddenly Simon found himself in a fight he hadn't started. He was just standing near two men who were at each other like it was the end of the world. And Simon, in a split second, decided that one of them had kinder eyes than the other. And he took sides. He was hailed as the saviour of the royal family because the one with the kinder eyes had been the future Prince. And Simon was promoted to the aristocracy. And the minute he had been promoted he learned that you could eat the cheese.

For three years he served under the prince out of respect for what he had given him. But then the prince died and Simon had no further allegiance. So he decided to tell the mice what had been kept from them for all of this time, they could eat the cheese. He thought it would free the common mouse from the tyranny with which they had been oppressed. But in the end it had lead to havoc.

Now nobody worked. Now all everyone did was eat the moon that they lived on. And now the moon was almost gone. The last great moonslip had happened a month ago when four thousand mice had slipped over the edge. The only person who could save them was Simon. He knew. He had to think of something...

But who could he turn to? The aristocratic mice weren't helping. Before when they had lived off the moon they had loved every fat second of it. But now they were going crazy. They still felt the need to show that they were better than the common mouse, and although Simon had tried to introduce other foodstuffs into the court as a way of stopping the slippages the rest of them were simply consuming more and more. Some of them had started melting down the cheese and bathing in it. This was simply the most preposterous idea Simon had ever heard in his life! They were bathing in cheese, which was dangerous in the first part because the

The book with the missing first page

temperature was so high, and then those mice that survived had to take a regular shower in one of the rain towers anyway.

But what could Simon do? The whole idea of a mouse utopia where every mouse could concentrate on higher things because they had enough food to eat had backfired. He had hoped not needing food would lead to scholarly works, instead of that they had all become lazy. It was terrible.

Simon picked up a piece of stilton and looked at it. He thought back to the world of his youth. Who could remember what life was like back then? After ten years of everyone eating cheese, after thirteen years of him eating cheese it was difficult to remember what it was like the very first time he had seen another mouse do it. But he could.

It was later in the day after he had helped the prince win in the fight. They hadn't really spoken about anything other than fighting and women. The prince was a dignified man in the correct social circles, but after that fight he was ready to talk as men do. Mainly he spoke about other fights and women, but he also mentioned drink and food. This last point interested Simon more than any other. Simon had a distinguished white spot in the middle of his back which had made him rather a success with the ladies, and so he wasn't much interested in conversations about how to get girls and what to do with them once he got them. But food was a different matter. Simon had never been truly able to apply himself. And he had always had to rely on the help of strangers. So food was always at the front of Simon's mind especially on that day as he hadn't eaten for a long time.

As Simon looked at this Stilton, this cheese that he had just picked up out of the ground, and was considering putting into his mouth he remembered just how far he had come.

How could he convince people to go back to something that they hadn't liked very much? That was the problem. In the old days when people hadn't had enough to eat it was a very personal problem, and now although everyone knew that eating the cheese was causing the whole moon to

Alex Andronov

fall away it was somebody else's problem. Simon knew that everybody thought that somebody else was going to solve it, and there was no motivation to bother. Because why bother to come up with a solution when eating the cheese right now isn't going to harm anyone. That was the problem, each slice of cheese wasn't hurting anyone by itself, it was just when everyone took a slice three or four times a day that they had started to run into trouble.

Simon realised that if anything was going to happen it would have to be him who solved the problem.

He thought about taxes or a way of rationing the cheese. Perhaps he could say that people could only have a slice after they had done a day of work. But how would you enforce it? The whole moon was made of cheese, they could just bend down while working and eat a piece? Or, more likely, just eat at home and not work.

If only there was some way of trying to cover the whole planet to stop them from getting at the cheese. But how would you do that? Maybe, Simon thought suddenly, he didn't need to stop them from getting at the cheese, what if he just made it so that they couldn't eat the cheese anymore? What if he could poison the cheese?

There was, in the armoury from the old days of war, huge vats of mouse poison. If he could get it into the source of the cheese then he would be able to stop everyone eating it. The cheese did grow a little bit each year. It grew out from the centre of the moon. The aristocracy had always kept it in check by eating enough, never more, never less than what was required to maintain the balance.

But how would he get to the core of the moon? That was going to be tricky itself. But Simon had an idea, he would appeal to the greed of the mice. He would tell them that the core of the planet was the greatest tasting cheese of all and that if they could dig down it would mean great cheese for those that had done it. He would have to get together a band of these Moon Miners, but he knew that the promise of tasty cheese and the

The book with the missing first page

rights to own the land down there would be enough to tempt them.

What he was doing would destroy the aristocracy as everyone would have to work, but he didn't mind that too much. Although he had now a new found respect for them as they knew better than he how to keep the moon in balance. But more than destroying the aristocracy, he would be destroying himself. There was no way he would survive. He'd be killed for sure.

Simon gathered together a large meeting of all of the leading mice, and announced that to save the moon they needed to re-establish the aristocracy. He told the selected mice that they deserved to be treated better than all of the other mice (to this he had great applause). But how would they be able to show to show their new status (at this muted grumbling about it had been his idea in the first place to tell everyone about the cheese)? He announced that he was going to tell them the last secret the prince had told him before he died. It was a secret so amazing that it would mean a way to re-establish the aristocracy. There was a way, he told them, to get to the centre of the moon where they would have access to the most fantastic, fresh cheese in the world. The cheese there would make normal moon cheese seem flat and tasteless and that they could have exclusive access to this cheese.

They agreed so rapidly that Simon thought it might even be a trap, but it wasn't. These powerful mice had been feeling so silly of late that they were completely desperate to re-establish their superiority.

So off they set and started digging. It was tough work, and these mice had never really done a day's work in their lives, so keeping them motivated was hard at first. But after a short while the cheese taste had improved so dramatically that the greedy mice were rushing to try and get back to the front of the digging party.

Simon bided his time, he knew that once they reached the fondue centre of the moon he would be ready, but until that time he would simply have to keep up the pretence.

Then finally, the big day came with a squeal of delight one of the mice had struck liquid cheese and it had oozed out all over his whiskers. They all kept digging around as Simon instructed until there was a wide opening, and Simon called out, "Bring the carrying barrels". They brought down the barrels of poison from the surface which Simon had told them were barrels for transporting the cheese up (he told them that they were reinforced to deal with the heat which is why they were so heavy). As they were set down on to a specially constructed platform which Simon had built himself he turned to the other mice around him and said, "You are my brothers, all of you but you are not friends of me or the moon. This place that was once so good has been destroyed by us all, and now one act of vandalism by me must restore the balance." And with this, before they could do anything about it, he pulled a special rope and all of the barrels went rolling straight into the centre of the moon. Each one melting in the sheer heat of the centre and releasing its deadly poison.

"I have poisoned the cheese, and although the cheese grows slowly, the poison will spread quickly. Within hours it will be too risky to take a bite and within two days all of the moon will be poisoned. You must all go back to your old ways of eating grain and working for a living. There is nothing you can do now to stop it, the moon will be saved. And if you ask me why I did it, I did it for our children." And with that Simon jumped into the molten cheese and instantly died.

The book with the missing first page

JENNA WAS NOT HAPPY

Jenna was not happy. She was not happy because two girls she thought liked her had not given her a Christmas card, even though they had spare ones on their desks and she walked past there three times.

Jenna was not happy because Wahkeen had been mean about her name. Which wasn't even fair because he was the one with the silly name. Having "Wahkeen Marine" as a name was a sign that your parents didn't really like you that much; Jenna was pretty sure of that. If they had even bothered to consult a dictionary and spell it Joaquin like everyone else, it might have seemed less like they were joking. So when he had run down the corridor in break shouting out "Jenna Jenna smells like henna" she had become mad. When all she had been able to come back with was "Well at least my name's spelt right", she had suddenly become decidedly not happy.

But most of all she was not happy because of something she had heard in the toilets. She had heard two older girls talking. One of them had been really excited about what Santa might bring her for Christmas. And the other girl had corrected her saying "you mean your parents." After a few seconds of explanation it had all been explained. The older girl thought Santa didn't exist. But the thing that was making Jenna not happy was that she was starting to believe it too.

The way Jenna saw it the alternative explanation seemed to make a lot more sense. Which, she wondered, was more likely? That an overweight man visited every child on exactly one night? Or that parents really gave the presents? Jenna knew what Uncle Occam would say.

Finally while thinking about all of this and looking thoroughly not happy her mother looked in the rear view mirror to check on her.

"Are you alright back there? You don't look very happy about something."
"No. I'm not happy. I'm not happy about three things."

Jenna was just about to go on and explain what the three things were but just then her mother started slowing down the car. So instead she said "Why are we slowing down?"

"Well there's a car just by the side of the road there which looks broken down. There's no other traffic around so I thought I'd better stop and check."
"Oh," said Jenna, "right."

Once the car was parked Jenna's mum got out and went to talk to the driver. Jenna couldn't see if it was anyone she knew because they were standing around the front of the car and the bonnet was up so that they could look at the engine.

She couldn't see but she might be able to hear if it was someone she knew. And just as she thought of that she heard the deep rumbling voice of a large man. But the voice had something else, something light and twinkling on top just so the rumbling wouldn't be so scary. Jenna only knew one person with a voice like that. But she didn't want to jump to any conclusions so she hopped out of the car and went to investigate. She slowly and carefully walked to the front of the car and when she got there she slowly and carefully peered around the corner.

Black boots. He had black boots! But so do lots of people Jenna thought.

Red trousers! But lots of people wear red trousers at Christmas time.

The book with the missing first page

A big silver buckle. Jenna decided with that that this looking slowly business wasn't all it was cracked up to be. She looked up and she saw Father Christmas.

"Santa!" she yelled.
Santa saw her and gave her a hug.

The rest of the conversation passed in a dream. And suddenly Jenna and her mother were back in their car driving home. But this time when Jenna's mum looked in the rear view mirror she could see Jenna had on the biggest grin of them all - the one she kept for very special occasions.

"It was a funny thing running into Santa like that wasn't it."
Jenna could only nod.
"He told me he was just off to the Mall."
"He was probably," Jenna said, "doing his Christmas shopping."
"Yes," said Jenna's mum, "he probably was."

Jenna thought to herself that this year Santa might need an extra mince pie. Even if she had only doubted him for a second, he might need one extra mince pie per second of doubt she'd had. Although as it hadn't been total doubt, maybe she'd try and get low fat mince pies.

Alex Andronov

IT'S THE NIGHT BEFORE THE NIGHT BEFORE HER WEDDING

It's the night before the night before her wedding. She comes home and throws the keys in the basket. Picks up the post off the mat. Flicks distractedly through it and wanders into the kitchen. She opens the fridge, finds some white wine from last night and pours it into a glass from the cupboard. Back to the fridge she takes some onions and garlic. At the board she starts to chop and slice the onions. With the garlic she takes the flat of the knife and smashes it onto the side of the garlic, some of her aggression flows with it. She smashes it again knowing that it doesn't really need it, she does it because it makes her feel better.

She takes pans from the cupboard, sips from the glass and slowly lets her day drift away on a cloud of routine cooking and alcohol. For a moment everything is calm but then a thought enters her mind and quick as a flash her hand flicks on Radio 4. No thinking and cooking, she's learned that doesn't work.

Midway through sautéing the onions he gets back, throws his keys in the basket, flicks through the post and turns on the tv. He's in there, she knows he is, because she can hear him flicking between channels. She wants him to acknowledge her and while she knows she could call out to him she lets him come to her.

The adverts come and he strolls into the kitchen leaving the tv on even though he knows it annoys her, he sidles up, gives her a kiss, steals some food, wanders off to the fridge for a beer and says, "so what's for dinner".

The book with the missing first page

"Are you sure you want to get married?", she asks matter-of-factly. She turns off Radio 4; she wasn't listening to it anyway.

"Not really."

He opens his can and takes a large swig. Looks at her and takes another one. She reaches for her wine and finishes the glass in one.

"No. Neither am I."

Alex Andronov

DOES THE NAME PAVLOV RING A BELL?

The beagle put out a cigarette and leaned back in his chair.

"What you've got to realise monkey is that we're here for the common good".
"Hey, my name is Albert."
"Albert," the beagle put forward a paw, "name's Boris, pleasure".
"Boris the Beagle - really?"
"You take the piss all you like, but I'm trying to help you. I could stop."
"Sorry. Sorry mate. Go on. Common good? Right? Right."
"Yeah. We go through all of this to help the humans and in return they give us some cigarettes."
"Aren't the cigarettes just another…"
"What?"
"Well… Nevermind. You actually like smoking."
"Me," Boris took another drag, "no. I don't smoke because I like it. I smoke because it makes me look cool. And anyway it beats the hell out of fox hunting."
"You don't enjoy the thrill of the chase?"
"I might, but I wouldn't know. I have the lung capacity of a gnat."
"But…"
"No really, they did a test. That's the current lung capacity I have - and I'm still alive. One day I hope, god willing, to get down to the lung capacity of dust."
"I don't think dust…"
"Yeah, then those guys down at the pound will have to give me respect."

YOU KNOW THE FEELING

You're sitting there reading this and you know that feeling like there is something on your ankle. Something that feels slightly heavy. Something attached. Like there's something crawling. Something slimey that's sliding up and over your ankle bump right now. Something that shouldn't be there. Something that doesn't know the difference between your leg and what it usually eats.

Do you know that feeling?

Alex Andronov

A MEETING IN THE PARK

Two men are sitting on a bench in the park on an incredibly hot summer's day. They are both wearing woollen suits and sunglasses. They even have the kind of hair that screams, "we are secret service operatives doing something dodgy".

There is no sign of contact between the two of them. The suggestion being that these two people wearing identically inappropriate clothing just happened to sit down next to each other. They have a newspaper sitting between them, the one who didn't put it down will pick it up before walking off. But before any of that can happen a single red balloon goes floating past them both.

They both break the thousand yard stares they've been practicing and look at it float gently past. The one closest to it jumps out of his seat and goes after it. It's floated a reasonable distance away by the time he's able to catch it. But when he does he doesn't head back to the bench. He just starts walking away.

Suddenly the seated suit jumps up, "Er, Simon, you've forgotten your paper."

"No Jonathan," says the balloon carrying Simon, "it's your turn to take the paper today".

"Oh sorry," says Jonathan, "getting up and taking the paper. It was that balloon, it completely distracted me."

The book with the missing first page

"Yes," says Simon, looking rather quizzically up at the balloon he is holding, "me too".

"Shall we try the museum tomorrow?"

"Fewer balloons"

"And less hot."

Alex Andronov

THE INFLUENZA ADVENTURE
A CITRON INVESTIGATION

I turned the corner and stopped. A bird on the floor. Why hadn't they found this one? Those fools, they'd been bodging this one from the start. I tapped the pigeon with the side of my boot. I could lift it off the ground easily enough. I stopped short of tipping it over, I could smell maggots. That had been all I wanted to know. It had been lying there for a while.

I walked closer and suddenly I saw what I had been expecting since I turned the corner. They looked like they had just been on a space ship with the suits that they were wearing or that they were dealing with some kind of nuclear spill. It all seemed slightly incongruous for Croydon.

One of them started bounding toward me. He was moving quite quickly, but he looked like he should have been moving in slow motion.

As he arrived near me I realised two things almost simultaneously. First that it was my good friend Geoffrey inside the suit and second that he had a second suit over his right arm.

"Hello Citron, how are things?"
"Things have, so far, been fine. Although, if you do try to make me wear that suit I will kill you."

I could see Geoffrey was looking me up and down and wondering which was the better thing in his life to be afraid of; me or his bosses. He already knew his answer but on some kind of whimsical off-chance he thought he should ask me just in case he could avoid trouble.

The book with the missing first page

"Wouldn't it be safer to wear it?"

"Perhaps it would, but that would have required me to have not stumbled over a dead bird at the end of the street and outside of the exclusion zone. This "would" has already gone wrong."

Geoffrey looked at me mournfully. He knew he would probably get in trouble for this. I saw there, loitering on his face, the understanding that he'd made the right decision. Knowing that he'd done it, I couldn't help but give him the excuse he needed.

"If it is bird 'flu I wouldn't need to be here. It wouldn't be a police matter until the contamination had been dealt with."

And with his reaction I had got my first information confirmed. I might have been called because somebody had purposely spread the bird 'flu.

But clearly something else was happening. The disease control people were starting to believe that it wasn't actually a disease. And that's why the bird had been left on the street. They were getting careless.

I followed Geoffrey as he led me back inside the restricted area. There were a couple of looks, as if people were saying that they half recognised me, that they half despised me, that they half wished that they too were able to not wear the ridiculous clothing and finally that they half realised that there had been too many halves by half.

A young man in spectacles walked up to Geoffrey and looked him up and down with an air of superiority. I was later to learn that this young pipsqueak was Geoffrey's boss and in a way had every right to look down upon poor Geoffrey. I mean I looked down on Geoffrey, but then I looked down on him as a friend, because I thought he would learn something from it. Whereas this looking down was done purely because it was a chance to be demeaning.

"What is *he* doing here?" said the pipsqueak to Geoffrey.
"Ah, Mr Cadeau, he is aiding us with our case."
"Why?"

"Why is he aiding us? That is quite a complicated question."
I decided to step in, "Ever since I was a child I was fascinated by the criminal mind."
"No", Cadeau said, "Why have you brought him in."
"You're on your own," I said, "I don't know yet."
Geoffrey stammered through a few apologies, and then I decided to put him out of his misery by offering to leave.
"No!" said Geoffrey and Cadeau at once. Cadeau continued, "I don't wish to inconvenience you Citron, that is all. But, please, I trust Geoffrey. I do. I know that if he has brought you here it must be for a good reason. I apologise for any inconvenience caused."

Cadeau literally clicked his heels together and pranced off. I turned to Geoffrey but before I could say anything he was saying, "Right, before you get a chance to say anything about my boss I need you to interview the key witness. She's had five people interview her already so she's not fresh, and she is tired."

Interviewing the witness was going to be interesting, she was hostile from the moment I walked in there. She did not want to be interviewed. But if there was information to be gained then I would be the man to gain it.

I walked into the house. Her house smelt fresh and clean but was not very warm. It smelt faintly of bleach. I wondered vaguely if she was an obsessive cleaner or if it was Special Branch who had been cleaning up during their evidence gathering. Or the often missed third option - both.

I was supposed to be interviewing this woman but why? I knew now that it was no longer a case of bird 'flu, but what was it instead? I could ask her, but presumably if she actually knew she'd have mentioned it already. I decided to go ahead. Since Cadeau hadn't seemed particularly keen for me to be here in the first place it would be best perhaps to at least aim for the impression of a normal investigation.

Her house was arranged unorthodoxly with her front room at the back,

The book with the missing first page

which led to my first question as I walked in.

"Unusual to find the front room at the back, wouldn't you say Ms…" I felt leaving things dangling was possibly the best way to get information.
"What is the purpose of this?" She said this in a voice that was not on directional volume; a voice that boomed in all directions. The purpose seemed to be to attract the attention of anyone other than myself to respond.
"Mr Citron is aiding us with our investigations," Geoffrey chipped in.

"Well what's the point of him? What about the other five men who have been in here. At least they seemed to have bothered to learn my name".
"W-W-Well," Geoffrey stammered, "your case has been being upgraded and moved around as we've got more information about it. We started by believing that your house was the epicentre of a case of bird 'flu. But now we think this isn't true. But unfortunately we don't know what it is now. Now that it has become an obscure non-contagious case we have brought in Mr Citron."

"Oh," she said, as though the matter had been settled some hours ago and that Geoffrey had been reiterating rather than revealing.

"So," I ventured, "Ms…"
"This lady is," Geoffrey started.
"This lady can speak for herself," she said on her own behalf, "I am Sarah Lockwinter. Miss Sarah Lockwinter. And you I notice are a Mr rather than a detective. Why is that."
"Ah," Geoffrey started.
"I too can speak for myself," I said stopping Geoffrey short, "I am a kind of contract worker. I only get brought in if the case is really strange and the police can't solve it. They don't always characterise it this way but it's true isn't it Geoffrey?"
"Yes, yes, it's true."
"I'm a gun for hire, but I do, just like those old-fashioned criminals, have certain principles."
"What are they?" she asked.

109

"Well, I never like to interview sober. What do you say to a drink?"

Sarah nodded at this, stood up from her couch and walked over to the drinks cabinet.

"Officer," she said to Geoffrey, "do you mind leaving us alone for a moment. I wouldn't like to put temptation in your path."
"Oh don't mind me," Geoffrey said.
"I do mind you, thanks," said Sarah, and with that she gave him a look so filthy that you would really have thought it would be a requirement to join a convent afterwards just to purge the spirit. It was a micro gesture but it was enough to convey to Geoffrey that he should back out of the room and wait until we were finished. And so that is exactly what Geoffrey did. He nodded at me just before he left. It was a nod asking for reassurance, I gave him none. It would have compromised me with the witness.

"So, Mr Citron, what's your poison?"
"Hmm, a slightly less original joke than you'd probably hoped."
"I'm sorry to hear that."
"Well, never mind. You weren't to know. I still get it less often than I get the offer of a squeeze of lemon. People like to say, 'Mr Citron, a squeeze of lemon?' which is particularly stupid because the drink I drink most often would curdle with such an addition and yet they say it to me anyway."
"So what's that?"
"What's what?"
"What's your usual drink?"
"Ah, a White Russian."
"That requires milk doesn't it."
"Yes."
"Sadly, the police have my milk."
"As evidence? But we know it's not 'flu now."
"No, for their tea."
"Ah."

There was suddenly a silence in the room. In fact this would have been the kind of situation where a breeze would have picked up to make a slight whistling sound if there had been one - but all of the windows were shut.

"So, what will it be?"
"I'll have whatever you're having."
"Okay then a gin and cranberry."
"Umm."
"You can have something else."
"No, no. A promise is a promise."

What had I let myself in for? I had been willing to accept any kind of regular alcohol and maybe tonic or water but to have fruit introduced was asking for trouble in my book.

She brought the drink over. It even had ice in it which she'd fished out of a plastic pineapple. I took a sip. It was immediately refreshing and then the after-taste made you feel more thirsty than you were at the start. It seemed like a dangerous kind of a drink. One that made you want more the more that you drank. Ye Gods!

I looked her in the eyes and said, "Tell me about your neighbour's cats."
"What?" she asked, as she looked surprised.

"What could my neighbour's cats have to do with anything?" Sarah asked.
"I am trying to decide that very question."
"So..."
"Well, although I hate cliche, 'if I knew the answer to that...'"
"Yes.?."
"Oh. The saying is, 'If I knew the answer to that, I wouldn't be asking the question'"
"So what have my neighbour's cats got to do with anything?"
"As I say, I'm not sure. Would you mind describing them for me."
"Well I don't know where to start."
"How about with their colourings."

Alex Andronov

"That's what I meant but she's got more than 10 cats. So I'm not really sure what they all look like. There's several tabbies, several pure black, at least one black one with a white underbelly. And so on, she has a lot of cats."

I looked around the room. It was an ordinary room. An ordinary living room. There were no clues in this room and yet I had seen the clue from the moment I had entered it. It wasn't in this room it was beyond it. It was in the garden. The most important two pieces of information were there to be watched on the real life television of her back window.

"When," I asked, "was the last time that your neighbour mentioned your bird feeder?"

"Oh, not for years now. It's verboten. We used to row about it all the time."

"Who originated the rows?"

"Well I did. Her cats keep trying to eat the poor birds. And I… I just don't think it's fair."

"So why have you stopped arguing about it? Have you suddenly become happy for her cats to eat the birds?"

"No. Not at all! She just wouldn't budge and neither would I. I knew that she'd never change and that we had to live next to each other so we both, about four years ago, decided that it was best to give it up. Give it up, ignore it, and just try to get along. It's worked much better."

"Until now."

"No, including now. We still haven't spoken about it since we made our pact."

"Just because you haven't spoken about it doesn't mean she hasn't been acting."

"What?"

"You know that cats are supposed to be being kept indoors during this bird 'flu crisis? Her cats aren't indoors even though she cares so much about them."

"What?"

I called out, "GEOFFREY!"

The book with the missing first page

Geoffrey walked back into the room.

"Yes Citron."
"Arrest the next door neighbour. Get forensics to check the bird feeder for poison. I can't believe you haven't done it already. The neighbour isn't a hardened criminal, she'll probably confess immediately."
They both said, "confess to what", at the same time.
"Confess to poisoning the bird feeder. She did it to protect her cats. She didn't want them to catch bird 'flu."
"Do you want to interview the neighbour?" Geoffrey asked.
"No. Why should I? I want to go and get a less dangerous drink."

And with that I got up, swished my coat tails behind me, and walked out of the room.

Alex Andronov

CAT'S EYES

He stepped out into the rain and already his hat had begun to get soaked through. He turned back towards the door to lock it. While his hand was returning the key to his pocket it brushed against a packet of cigarettes. It was a difficult choice. He could light it here, but would it go soggy out in the rain? He had no choice, once his hand felt the pack he had to light one. The air was so damp that the first two strikes of the match failed to take. He chuckled to himself as the third time lit true, with him it wasn't three strikes and out.

He turned back out into the rain and that's when he saw the cat. It was just sitting there staring back at him. A cat which probably would have looked cute sprawled on the grass in the sunshine, but tonight it looked back at him with those reflective eyes. It looked back at him and it seemed to know something. He wanted to just walk past it, but he froze, just staring at it, staring at it staring at him.

The cat got up and started walking towards him. Just as it was about to walk past it turned and gave him one last look, and then it walked on.

He stepped forward and then stopped. Water actually sloshed off his hat and onto his feet. He hadn't meant to stop, not in the rain. But he found that he was suddenly unsure of himself. This deal was too important to miss. If he didn't come through the consequences would be terrible. But somehow, something made him stop. Something made him stop out there in the rain. He turned back, unlocked the door, and stepped back in. The cat had unnerved him.

TRAPPED

It's dark. You can't see. Your arms and legs move sluggishly because of the weight of the water on them. You almost start thrashing about just to get some freedom but as soon as you start you remind yourself to stop. To be calm. To concentrate on keeping your head above the water. You can feel the line around your neck like a noose. It's rising. It's rising quite quickly now. You tilt your head and that keeps your chin out of the water. You keep kicking with your legs, keep kicking, keep trying to stay afloat, keep kicking. And your hands are constantly searching, constantly tracing along the surface of the roof, the roof that you're getting far too close to. Your hands feel only the smooth metallic surface. You know there is nothing. No release. Now no matter how you angle your head your chin is under water. You can't move to keep searching. Your legs are tired but you keep kicking. Water laps against the corner of your lips. Even with your mouth closed you can feel it creeping into the cracks of the corners. You know it's too dark to see anything but you have to try something. You turn and swim underwater, hands outstretched, blind, searching. It's the last thing you remember.

Alex Andronov

"I THINK THAT'S PROBABLY IT FOR ME"

"I think that's probably it for me", Paul turned to his left and put out his cigarette in his beer. It flew in at an angle with a hiss and stuck to the side of the glass. A bearded drunk from two stools down looked on at the waste of beer with a mixture of disgust and calculated longing as though he was asking himself the question, "how much do I hate my insides right now?"

Paul hopped off the stool with more composure than a man who has been in a bar all night should have. He looked to his companion and asked the question she'd been waiting for all night, "do you want to come back with me and see my etchings"?

She nervously laughed and smiled, this was it she thought. She could become a hero tonight - if only she kept playing it cool - she instantly remembered herself and tried to forget the seven gins and tonic* she had drunk. She tottered off her stool, but in a calculated way so that she was slightly off-balance on her heels. She was exactly as off-balance as she needed to be so that he could catch her if he was suave enough but that if he didn't notice she wouldn't fall flat on her face.

He noticed and rebalanced her. She laughed and flicked her head back so that he saw her smile, her cleavage heave and so that her hair just barely brushed against his ear. He grinned and said, "okay, let's get in that cab".

They walked outside and the cool air cleared their heads faster than a turd clears a swimming pool. A taxi was floating past, Paul whistled and she

The book with the missing first page

put her hand out. The cab stopped and Paul whispered, and then shouted, his address to the mildly deaf taxi driver. They got in and squeaked into the leatherette seats while the soothing sounds of the Eagles played havoc with their emotions.

They drove for what felt like ten minutes and eleven minutes later they were standing outside Paul's place.

"Would you like to come up?" Paul knew exactly what to say.
"Yes," she said, "I've always been fascinated to see a loft apartment".
"Well don't get too excited, it's just like any other kind of place".
"Except," she whispered into his ear, "that it's at the top of the pile. Kinda like you Paul".

They both walked up the stairs uneventfully, and as they reached the top Paul turned and said, "this is it".

Martha took her gun from her purse, pointed it at Paul, and said, "in a very real sense, that's true".

Paul, keeping his cool like a Amcor AMC 10000 Air Conditioning unit**, simply said "If you shoot me then I'll be dead, and you'll never see those etchings, those etchings are under lock and key, and you don't have the key and you don't even know where the lock is, in fact even if you put that key in that lock which you'd happened to find then you'd still have problems as you'd have to type a sixteen digit code into a box which doesn't even look like it accepts codes typed into it, and then you'd have to speak into a microphone a special phrase that you don't know using my voice that you won't have and then when you finally see those etchings, those etchings that you so desire that you're willing to kill for them, you won't understand them because you won't have me to explain that they have been influenced by a number of great artists that I don't care to mention right now because if I don't mention them then you'll have slightly less reason to kill me. And that, amongst many other reasons, is why you shouldn't kill me". And he said all of that before he realised that all of the things that he'd had to say had been a little more complicated than he'd

Alex Andronov

intended at the start of his simple sentence.

Martha lit a cigarette with her gun-shaped lighter, tilted her head back and laughed a laugh which seemed to say "why does it all have to be so complicated?", but actually she said in verse:

"Paul, your etchings sound lovely,
they really do,
but to see them sounds complicated,
so shall we just screw".

* I know it looks weird, but it is right.

** ***

*** I honestly haven't been paid any money by them, I just put "air conditioning unit" into google and clicked on the first link that came up and ranked the resulting units by rating and picked the first one.

The book with the missing first page

IN MY KITCHEN

The salt skittered across the kitchen counter and mingled with the rosemary and pepper that were already lying there - spoils of cooking. The chicken looked pale next to the black roasting tin, but soon would be coloured by the oil and spices that were being prepared in a small mortar. The pestle is rammed in and the herbs give up their essential oils. The mess around the preparation area builds as more boards are used and things are chopped.

Jenny stops adding to it for a second and decides to clear down her station. Even though this is her own kitchen in her own house she still thinks of it as a station in a fancy restaurant that she wishes she ran. Michael is watching the football in the living room and the sound is way up. He won't be able to hear her. She walks over to the kitchen door and closes it a bit more.

She takes a swig of her Sauvignon Blanc and starts to commentate, just audibly. "It is always important to keep your station clear. Although don't worry too much if you make a mess as you're going along. After all this is supposed to be fun. But do try and not to let it get too far away from you." She finished wiping down the counter with a paper towel and threw it in the bin.

"Now what you need to do is make sure your hands are good and clean because we're going to rub the suffusion we've made onto the chicken skin."

Alex Andronov

Just as she's saying this the door opens, Michael walks in and starts rummaging around in the fridge for another beer. "Who were you talking to?" he wants to know.

"Nobody," says Jenny.

The book with the missing first page

SARAH

There was one tiny wisp of a grey cloud on a blue sky. The rest were all pure white and on the blue sky they seemed like they had tumbled out of a kind of airline or washing powder commercial.

Sarah was lying face down on the grass, craning her neck up at them. She had a book in front of her but she was ignoring it. Every time she thought about reading it and looked down she had to adjust her eyes to the darkness. The brilliance of the sky was so different from the dull grey pages of her book. Why do the most interesting people insist on living in books? she wondered. More to the point, why did they always seem to be in the most boring dullest old books that smelt of damp? Sarah slammed the book shut, picked it up and threw it into her rucksack.

She rolled over so she had her back on the grass and looked at the sky. It was blue all around her. She imagined for a second that she was floating in the sea and it felt glorious. She waved her arms through the lush long grass and felt how soft it was, the smell of fresh grass interfered with her vision partially but she over-rode it because she loved it so much. She lost herself while she swam a kind of upside-down breast stroke through the grass. She opened her eyes again and saw the clouds above her. Her mind wondered what they were. What could they be floating in the sea? They must be icebergs she imagined and it made her physically shiver. She closed her eyes again but the moment was gone, she knew she was lying on a hill near her house. And that nothing, nothing ever happened within a thousand miles of her house.

Alex Andronov

"Um, excuse me?"

Sarah didn't know what to do. A man had just addressed her. She didn't know what she was supposed to do in this situation. She supposed she must first open her eyes. Perhaps. She put that thought on hold and decided that before she saw him the proper thing would be to adjust her hair. She didn't want to be obviously doing it after she saw that he was beautiful - that would look desperate. She pushed her hand through her fringe, pulled herself up, so that she was in an L-shape and then adjusted the back of her hair. And then she opened her eyes and saw him.

As she looked up and saw him she could see... he was beautiful. Not rugged or handsome but beautiful. He had an aquiline nose and blonde, slightly longer than regulation, hair. It rustled in front of her as he bent towards her, and seemed to frame a halo above him.

"Who are you?", she asked.
"Oh," he said, slightly straightening back up, "my name is Steven Shaw".
"That sounds like a name out of an adventure book"
"It does rather, doesn't it? Well I think I'm on the right track then".
"What do you mean?," Sarah asked.
"Well adventuring is kind of what I do," he paused for a second as though realising the lack of sense he might be making but then added, "for a living", which didn't really help.

Sarah pushed herself up off of her back and supported herself on her arms. She looked at him for a bit and wondered what she made of him. She decided to push on rather than telling him to get lost.

"What are you doing here?"
"I live here when I'm not travelling. Well, not here in this field, but just down the hill. So what do you do?"
"I... I... I don't seem to do much of anything."
"Nothing?"
"Nothing much."

The book with the missing first page

Sarah wondered why she had said that. She had suddenly felt what she did was less important somehow. That what she did was somehow less than what?

"How can you be an adventurer?," she asked, "they don't exist."
"They do in your book," he gestured to where it lay beside Sarah.

She looked down at it, it had been well-loved and was slightly frayed at the edges. It looked really pretty folded open, sitting in amongst the blades of grass. She wished she had had her camera with her. She looked up at the man suddenly remembering something. He had a Polaroid camera slung round his neck.

"Do you think you could take a picture of my book in the grass? It looks so lovely lying there."
"Of course," he replied and he quickly crouched down beside her to get close enough to take the picture.

Sarah could smell his scent now which was a delicate mix of sandalwood and musk. He carefully took the picture and the click-wurr action of the camera did the rest. He carefully held the emerging picture with one hand while letting the camera fall back to his side with the other. He passed the picture to her. She waved it vaguely in the warm air. Then she looked at it. It really had captured the colours well. She picked up her book and placed the photograph in between the pages making it into an impromptu book mark.

She looked back up at him. She could see, now that she was this close, that his bright blue eyes were flecked with grey.

"So how can you be an adventurer?"
He held out his hand and said, "let me explain in the pub".
She looked around. Until he had suggested it she had felt utterly content. But now she realised that she was actually quite thirsty. "Okay," she said, "but where?"
"Don't worry," he replied while helping her up, "follow me".

Alex Andronov

Sarah had never walked this way down the hill before. She'd always meant to but once she'd got to the top of the hill she'd always stopped there. It was always as though a piece of elastic was tying her to home. But while it was strange, Sarah was quietly relieved. She hadn't wanted to walk into a pub with this guy and find a bunch of her friends there instantly judging him. She wasn't ready to share him yet.

They walked down the hill in near silence. Sarah could hear a bird twittering. Sarah always imagined when she heard this particular kind of bird that it was making cat calls at her. Like there was a group of builder birds who said things like, "oh yes we'll build your nest extension and bird bath for you obviously, but that birch twig finish you're after Mrs Robin… It'll cost ya extra". She imagined that these builder birds whistled at her but she thought it might sound a little mad and so she didn't mention it to Steven.

The ground started to level out and soon they were walking on a country lane. There was a distinct smell of tilled earth mixed with the unmistakable pong of manure. Luckily this passed after a second. Steven paused for a moment, took in an artificially deep breath and said, "Ah, I love the smells of the countryside. Now if I'm not mistaken the pub must be just around this corner".

Steven picked up his pace and Sarah followed. There, as promised, was the pub. It was an old stone building with flowers in hanging baskets. The only thing missing, Sarah thought, was a beer garden. Steven walked up to the door, opened it and stepped inside - holding the door open behind him. Sarah walked in behind him. She hadn't been sure about the idea of going to the pub the whole time she'd been walking down the hill. Sarah couldn't quite see how going to the pub seemed very adventurer-ish. As she was actually crossing the threshold she suddenly wondered what kind of drink he would have.

Sarah walked past Steven and into the pub. It had a cold stone floor which made the room feel very refreshing after the heat of the sunshine and the walk down the hill. She walked forward towards the bar and couldn't

The book with the missing first page

help but notice that bartender only had one arm. Steven was right behind her, he walked closer to the bartender and said, "a pint of Guinness and a packet of peanuts please Pete".

Pete looked over at Sarah, "what'll it be for you missy?"

He didn't wait for her, he'd already started moving over towards the Guinness pump. There was a "clack" on every alternate step - clearly Pete only had one leg as well. Sarah realised she was staring at him a little bit, and she looked round to Steven. Steven looked at her and smiled.

"Interested in old Pete eh? You're right to be, he's an interesting fellow Pete."
"Urgh," said Pete.
"You're being too modest Pete. Pete used to be an adventurer too. Sadly he got a little bit too friendly with a crocodile. Now he serves drinks for a living."
"And peanuts," says Pete.
"What," asked Steven, "would you like? I'd recommend the Guinness."
"I don't really like Guinness I'm afraid."
"Ah, well then you better try something else. I never have so I can't really recommend anything."
"Can I have a whiskey?"
"Urgh"

Pete walked towards the side of the bar and found a stool. He carried it back and started to climb on it and then, after steadying himself, reached up and plucked a bottle of whiskey off of the top shelf. He took out two glasses. Poured a large measure into both and then put the bottle back and kicked the stool out of the way. He picked up both of the glasses and thrust one towards Sarah. And then, looking at the other glass he said, "well I may as well toast a lassie who likes whiskey. Cheers."

Steven managed to rescue his stout from the wrong side of the bar where it had been settling and they all toasted Sarah - even though Sarah seemed a tad confused by the whole thing. Pete took the end of the toast

125

Alex Andronov

as a signal to shuffle off again and Steven tipped his head in the direction of a table in the corner of the room.

As they walked towards the table Sarah realised that it wasn't quite a corner. The room wasn't quite square and the table was in a little corridor. As they sat at the table Sarah found she was facing away from the main pub, she was looking down the corridor at a closed door.

"So," said Steven.
"So," said Sarah.
"Yes?"
"Yes. I…"
"What? Go on…"
"I," said Sarah, "I was going to say, I was going to say the whole way down the hill that going to the pub didn't feel like going on an adventure. But now I'm not so sure. I hadn't expected Pete for a start."

"No, not many people expect Pete."
"And to an extent it's an adventure for me simply because I've never been on this side of the hill, and here I am with a strange man, but for you it isn't really an adventure is it? You've been on this side of the hill before, you've been to this pub before, drunk that Guinness."
"Well not this particular pint of Guinness no, but would you be trying to claim with all of that that you aren't a strange girl?"
"I'm not strange. I'm perfectly normal."
"Ha."
"I am. I'm boring."
"I don't believe that. You might be bored but you're not boring."
"Can't you be both?"
"People can, but not you. Your mind is too inquisitive."

As he had been speaking Sarah had been noticing that a light behind the door was getting brighter and brighter. She was about to say something but then Steven said, "How many people do you think imagine birds are wolf-whistling at them?"

The book with the missing first page

"What?" Sarah said, the light was getting brighter, but she couldn't ignore what Steven had just said. "How could you know that?"
"I can't tell you that for a moment. But it's true isn't it."
"Yes."

"Things like that make you interesting. You never tell anyone about it because you fear what people might think of you. What you don't realise is that admitting to the interesting things about you might make people more interested in you, rather than less."

Sarah could hardly ignore the door now. Bright white light was shining all around it and through the keyhole. Rays were dancing on the ceiling and floor, patterns on the walls and the light switch were so bright they were difficult to look at. She looked back at Steven.

"Ignore the door."
"But?"
"Just for a moment."
"But!"
"Admit that you are interesting and you don't need something to happen to you to prove it."
"Steven."
"Ignore the door."

Sarah looked straight at Steven. His blue eyes really were amazingly bright, even in the relative darkness compared to what she had just been looking at. What had she been looking at? She faltered for a second wanting to look back at the door. But she could see in Steven's eyes a pleading for her not to look.

"Okay," she said, "I admit it. I am more interesting than I normally admit."
"Good then," said Steven, "now you are ready to decide. Do you want to go through the door?"

Sarah looked at the door. The light was doing strange things now. It looked like the door was bulging out towards her. She looked back at Steven.

"What should I do?"
"That's what you have to decide."
"But I'm scared. I think I should just go home. I'm sorry."
"Don't be sorry. I just thought you wanted to go on an adventure."
"I do, but I want to know what's going to happen. I want to know what to expect."
"But," said Steven, "that's not an adventure then, is it? That's like a theme park ride."

Sarah looked at Steven. His bright blue eyes were looking very deeply into hers. He seemed to be half imploring her to go and half upset to be having to explain everything.

Sarah didn't know what to do. She looked down at the table. Every normal, sensible part of her brain was telling her to flee. But there was something so desperately fascinating about the door. She got up and walked towards it. The ground seemed to be getting hotter and hotter as she got closer and closer to the door. She worried for a second about touching the metal handle. So she pulled her sleeve down over her hand and opened the door. The white light flooded the whole room. Sarah could hardly look forward. But she stepped gingerly over the threshold. And the door slammed behind her. Steven wasn't with her.

Sarah turned and she realised that she couldn't see anything. Everything in all directions was white. She closed her eyes and opened them. Nothing had changed. She closed her eyes again and held them closed for longer. The light was so bright that even having her eyes closed didn't seem to make much of a difference. Everything was simply pink instead of white.

Sarah could suddenly feel something soft on her back. And a breeze. Some slight breeze was curling across her face. She opened her eyes and she realised she was back in the field lying in the grass. Sarah felt like

The book with the missing first page

she'd just woken up. It couldn't have been a dream, thought Sarah. It had seemed far too real for that. She'd had vivid dreams before but only quick moments nothing as sustained as this.

Sarah couldn't believe that it had only been a dream. It was so disappointing. She stood up. Deciding to go back home. As she picked up her book something fell out and landed on the grass. It was the picture Steven had taken of her book. And on the bottom in the white section there was some writing:

"Choosing to go through the door means that you're ready. I'll come and fetch you in a few days. P.T.O."

Sarah turned over the polaroid and on the bottom of this side it said:

"By the way you've been spelling my name wrong in your mind.
Love,
Stephen Shawe".

Sarah walked down the hill not knowing what to expect next.

Alex Andronov

IMPORTANT AT THE TIME

She pulled apart her scrapbook some years ago. At the time there had been a point to it. She had needed the pictures, the postcards for something. Whatever it had been, it had obviously seemed important at the time.

Important at the time. This book had once been important at the time. She had won a prize for it. It had been the best one. And now there were just the echoes of the book itself. The one line notes. The coloured-in map. And the holes that stared back at her. The glue, unseen to her as it had been smushed up behind the pictures, had formed into little streaks which looked now like tears. As though the book had cried when it had been ripped apart.

She realised that she had been holding her breath while she had been thinking about it. She exhaled and the breeze she produced moved a piece of tissue paper. She took the paper and wrapped the book back up in it.

She wouldn't have to cry if she hid the book away again. She hid the book. And cried anyway.

The book with the missing first page

JAKE TURNWEED

Jake Turnweed was walking. What? Isn't that enough for you people? No? Oh I'm sorry. I do apologise. I hadn't realised that it was your story. So go on then. Do continue. Write the next bit yourself.

"Ummmm."

No? It's not so easy, is it?

"But I don't…"

Oh don't give me that "you don't know what actually happened next" crap. He walked to school, didn't he?

"Jake Turnweed walked to school"

Oh, very clever. Very smart. I'm not impressed, you know. I have absolutely no reason to be impressed. For that transgression I'm not telling you the rest of the story. See if I care.

Printed in the United Kingdom
by Lightning Source UK Ltd.
126314UK00002B/287/A